To Thomas Belle 4th IV
(Motie)

SUPREME BEINGZ:
FINDING THE INNER G

Thank you for your
support!

DT

SUPREME BEINGZ:

Finding the Inner G

2nd Edition

BY DAMON THOMPSON

Charleston, SC
www.PalmettoPublishing.com

Supreme Beingz
Copyright © 2022 by Damon Thompson

All rights reserved

Second Edition

Hardcover ISBN: 978-1-68515-478-3
Paperback ISBN: 978-1-68515-479-0
eBook ISBN: 978-1-68515-480-6

Disclaimer
This is a fictional story. Most of the characters and names are the product of the author's imagination. Any resemblance to actual persons is from the author's experience.

TABLE OF CONTENTS

ACKNOWLEDGMENTS

This book is dedicated to Andrew and Florence Singleton, my loving grandparents. I love you dearly, thank you for setting the foundation by providing the love and protection that we all needed for our development. The house that is displayed on the back of this book is where my childhood began, and imagination was sparked. Thank you so much, grandmama and granddaddy for opening your home to all your children and grandchildren.

Chapter 1:

FRIDAY INDIVIDUAL THERAPY SESSION

1:00 pm Session

As the two started the session, Mrs. Davenport was very perturbed and nervous. Her smile was insecure with clear lip gloss painted neatly. Her left hand moved in a wave motion as she massaged her thigh up and down. The sun rays that maneuvered through the window allowed her ring to shine, which complimented each diamond. Staxx seemed relaxed and poised. He was wearing slim fit pants with a cardigan sweater where he kept his belongings. He took off his glasses and began to clean them with a cloth that he pulled out of his top right pocket.

"So, Mrs. Davenport, how are you doing today?" Staxx asked.

Mrs. Davenport was wearing gym attire that complimented her body. She removed her purse from her arm and placed it on the chair to the left of her.

"I'm doing okay. I have had better days, you know?" she answered.

"I see," Staxx replied. "So, tell me, how are things going at home with Mr. Davenport. Has he made a decision to join you with sessions?"

Staxx was attempting to use an open-ended question to engage in a dialogue that would allow Mrs. Davenport to open but calm down. She took a long exhale, smiled, and then giggled.

"I'm doing the best I can do to keep this marriage together. I cook, clean, wash his clothes, and all of my duties as a stay-at-home wife," she explained.

Staxx continued his questioning. "Are you and Mr. Davenport working on the activities?"

"Yes." Mrs. Davenport began. "However, it is difficult when he feels that he doesn't need help or therapy. He's very old school," she giggled.

"Tell me more concerning Mr. Davenport being old school," encouraged Staxx.

Mrs. Davenport loved to discuss the issues concerning her husband, but it was difficult for her to touch the issues that she was dealing with internally.

"My husband is older than me…like 20 years older. He is a traditional man that believes his wife should take care of the home while he works, protects, and provides. Counseling or therapy is like telling him something is wrong with him, or he isn't doing something right. He also feels that marriage therapy is just going to put people in his business." Mrs. Davenport explained passionately.

"So how does he feel about you attending these sessions without him?" Staxx asked.

"Well…" she began, "He said if it's going to help me then he will pay for it, but he's not attending."

"I understand." Staxx replied as he pondered on his thoughts. "I really would like to meet him and propose a different way of thinking".

At that moment, Staxx realized that the age difference between this couple could be what was causing the disconnection within their marriage. He went on to inquire how the two met.

"We met two years ago at the gym. He was and still is a charmer." said Mrs. Davenport. "He became my personal trainer and helped me to establish a healthy lifestyle. We began dating, and after a year he proposed."

"So, I assume you noticed an age difference between the two of you?" Staxx inquired.

"Yeah, I noticed there was an age difference, but to be honest, that is what made me more attracted to him. It was kind of like the freshman dating a senior in college." she said while blushing.

As the session continued, Staxx traveled with Mrs. Davenport through her memories as she went into full detail about how Thomas proposed to her.

"It was my birthday, and he had this amazing weekend planned," she began. "He called my job prior to my birthday and informed my boss that I would not be in. He picked me up from my place and all he would tell me is that we were going on a trip. I didn't have any bags packed so I was confused and anxious. He told me that we would go shopping once we got to our destination. We went to the mountains in Asheville, North Carolina, a place where he knew I always wanted to visit. He proposed during dinner. It was so lovely." she affirmed as she slowly drifted back to reality.

"So, it seems like Mr. Davenport put some major thought into his proposal to you and genuinely displayed that he really wanted to make you happy," Staxx confirmed.

Before she could respond, Mrs. Davenport's phone rang. She looked at the phone unconcerned and declined the call.

"Excuse me, I should have turned this on vibrate," she said, embarrassed.

"No problem," Staxx replied.

As the session continued, Staxx attempted to read Mrs. Davenport's thoughts. He placed his index finger on his right temple in the thinking mode. Thoughts of her husband flooded Mrs.

3

Davenport's mind and roamed freely no matter how hard she tried to block them.

Staxx could see her body reacting to her thoughts. "Is everything okay?" he asked.

"Yes, I'm okay. Just thinking about my to-do list for the day." Mrs. Davenport responded with a small tremble in her voice.

Staxx glanced down and noticed there was a message from her husband that read "Where Are You?" Her phone started to vibrate.

"Maybe you should go ahead and answer that," Staxx suggested.

Mrs. Davenport declined the call and turned her phone off.

"There! That should take care of that," she said right before she released a long sigh.

Staxx began to have an uneasy feeling. "Maybe we should reschedule for a later date and pick up from here."

"No, no, no, no, no!" Mrs. Davenport quickly responded. "We should continue the session. I really need to get something off my chest that has been troubling me for quite a while now."

Staxx recognized he needed to hear Mrs. Davenport out if he ever wanted to gain her trust and make her comfortable enough to freely discuss her issues.

Staxx's assistant Lauryn knocked at the door subtly.

"Yes, Lauryn. Please come in," Staxx instructed.

"Sorry to interrupt," Lauryn began. "But you received a call from a Mr. Davenport. He said it was urgent that he speak with you. I told him that you were busy, but he insisted that you give him a call sooner than later. You also received a call from Big Geechie, he said give him a call," Lauryn explained.

Mrs. Davenport's eyes stretched wide open, catching Staxx's attention.

"Did Mr. Davenport leave a contact number?" asked Staxx.

"Yes, I have it here," Lauryn answered as she gave the sticky note with the phone number written on it to Staxx.

He looked at the number and then thanked Lauryn. Lauryn walked out with a concerned look on her face.

"You really should call your husband. It could be an emergency," Staxx pleaded.

She pulled out her phone and turned it back on. She had three new messages in her inbox. Staxx used his telekinesis powers to listened to all three of the messages before Mrs. Davenport could get to them. The messages were her husband reminding her that she better not be at the shrink's office.

Mrs. Davenport insisted that they continue with the session, but Staxx informed her that the session would have to end.

Mrs. Davenport was not in the mood to be compromising or polite and proceeded to demand that they finish the session. She needed to finish discussing her concern regarding her husband and she needed to do it that day.

With her hands covering her head she screamed, "I can't take it anymore!"

Tears trickled down her cheeks slowly. Staxx offered her a tissue from a box on the table.

"Thank you," she managed to force out through her tears. She used the tissue to wipe away her tears, smearing her makeup in the process.

She reiterated, "I JUST CAN'T!" She continued wiping tears from under her eyes and off her cheeks.

"Mrs. Davenport, I need you to be totally honest with me about you and your husband. Does your husband know that you are taking therapy sessions?" Staxx gently inquired.

"Why does it matter?" questioned Mrs. Davenport.

"It matters because that could seem disrespectful and deceitful to him. Also, potentially very dangerous for you," he explained.

As she soaked in the reality of what Staxx was trying to explain, she felt she needed to discuss her intentions going into her marriage.

"I never wanted this to happen!" Mrs. Davenport explained. "I am a great wife to Thomas! I never disrespected him in any form or fashion. All I want for him to do is stop being so jealous and just trust me!"

Staxx's interest peaked. "Why do you feel like your husband doesn't trust you?"

"Before I got married, I had a social life and lots of friends. Now I'm just stuck in the house doing things that he labels a wife's duty! My girls and I would go into the city on some weekends and enjoy the nightlife. It's going on a year since I've been able to have fun with them. I really feel like I don't know who I am anymore. Just the thought of me having children makes my stomachache. I would be trapped. I never thought I would miss my job. Now I see that working there was my passion, and it gave me a purpose to pursue. He has truly destroyed my dreams of becoming what I always wanted to be!"

"What is that?" Staxx asked.

"A singer and songwriter!" Mrs. Davenport answered with a totally different tone and energy. "I love singing and writing songs. It gives a recharge and fresh life."

"Maybe you should write a song about what you are going through in your marriage," suggested Staxx.

"Wow. I never thought of that," replied Mrs. Davenport, shaking her head. "That's not a bad idea, but I'm sure he will find a way to snatch my soul right away from me."

As Mrs. Davenport continued to address her dreams and aspirations, Staxx listened closely to the feelings and emotions that she was expressing. He could feel everything that was being expressed and knew it was true and sincere.

Mrs. Davenport's tears of agony had turned into tears of joy as she thought about her dreams.

Staxx continued to encourage her to write about her experiences. He explained, "Several artists write their best work when they are going through challenging tribulations."

Staxx was interrupted by Mrs. Davenport once she realized that she had totally forgotten to call her husband back. She quickly pulled out her phone and called him. The phone rang several times before going to his voicemail. She called him again. The voicemail came on after several rings.

"Hi. You've reached Thomas. I'm sorry I'm not available, but if you would leave a message and number, I will get back with you. Have a blessed day."

Mrs. Davenport looked puzzled. It was not like Thomas to not answer his phone.

"He must be in the shower," she said nervously.

"So where did you work before you got married?" Staxx inquired.

Mrs. Davenport snapped out of her daze and responded, "I worked at The Arts and Science Charter School as a music and culture teacher."

Staxx paused for several seconds. "The Arts and Science school on Garden Lane?" Staxx asked.

"Yes! The one on Garden Lane!" she confirmed.

"Wow. What a small world," he said in astonishment, leaving Mrs. Davenport curious about what he meant.

Staxx went on to explain: "I heard great things about ASC and the talented kids there."

Mrs. Davenport expressed her love for teaching the students about different cultures and the different types of music within them. She felt so much guilt and as if she did the students a disservice by quitting.

"It really didn't feel like a job. I really loved working there and I was really stupid for leaving that place," she explained. "Teaching those kids about writing music to embody the culture in which they originated made me feel like I was fulfilling my passion."

"You should really discuss your passion about your former job with your husband. That may trigger some emotions and allow him to empathize with you," said Staxx.

Mrs. Davenport continued to share her experiences, totally disregarding what Staxx said. "I can recall this one student that was gifted beyond measure. He would write the most interesting poems and songs. He was very knowledgeable about social issues. He was also a student-athlete. He got caught up in the wrong crowd and eventually dropped out of school."

"I am sorry to hear that," Staxx replied. "It sounds like he could have done great work in the world. That story you just shared can be a song or poem for you to write about. Mrs. Davenport, what I am trying to persuade you to do is tap into your creative side. You are a brilliant woman. You have a pure soul that is rare in today's world. Your life experience should be shared in an art form which would allow other creative minds to relate to your experience."

Mrs. Davenport sat there with an inspired look embedded in her face and was overpowered by a feeling like she had never felt. She started tearing up...AGAIN. This time, they were tears of inspiration and motivation. Mrs. Davenport heard what she needed to hear in her marriage, support.

"If only these words came from my husband," she said.

They both heard a loud scream from a woman and looked back to see where the noise was coming from. Then the earth-shattering sound of a machine gun clip was inserted, and an array of bullets sounded off. Windows shattered and paper on the desk flew in the air and slowly made its way to the floor like confetti. Pictures and frames fell off the wall and instantly shattered once they contacted the floor.

Staxx pushed Mrs. Davenport down to the floor causing her body to jerk from the force of the push. Mrs. Davenport screamed as she curled into the fetal position, covering her ears. Staxx heard another clip inserted as the person reloaded the gun. Bullets began to travel through the window and door with tenacity.

The shooting stopped and footsteps came down the hall. Sounds of the perpetrator's boots stepping on shattered glass turned subtle. Everything became silent. The building door slammed, a vehicle door opened, and the tires shrieked as they gained momentum, digging into the pavement as the car sped from the parking lot.

Chapter 2:

DOC'S PRAYER

5:00 A.M. group text message

Wake up! Wake up! Wake up! LET'S GET IT!

Several messages replied. "I'm on it!" "I've been up. You're late." Myles replied, "It's too early. Go back to sleep."

Staxx always sent a morning text to the fellas to remind them to work out in the gym. They have a very close bond. They always look out for one another, just as Doc taught them. Doc is the grandfather of Staxx and all the guys in his group text.

Staxx is a routine guy. Every morning was the same thing. Meditate, pray, workout, and eat. Music was the glue that kept the brethren's bond tight. They would talk about hip-hop for hours on the phone or via text message. Somehow, some way music was involved in all of their lives. Whether it is Myles implementing a lesson plan of hip-hop at his school where he was a chemistry teacher, or Seven listening to Wu-Tang Clan on a plane as he traveled to Africa. They all are from Beaufort, South Carolina, home of a rich Gullah culture, blood of runaway slaves, and hearts of kings.

Beaufort was the place where the guys grew up and received their life jewels from Doc. At some point in their life, all of them stayed at their grandparents' home where they received blessings over their lives.

Doc is not a religious man; however, he is very spiritual. He would spend hours talking to God discussing the desires of his heart. He would delight himself in the eyes of God. Doc always taught his grandkids to seek God's presence. Whether it be taking early morning walks and absorbing nature or talking to God for guidance (prayer), Doc always instilled in his grandchildren that they all were blessed by God with special gifts and they must use them for good. Each grandchild was blessed with something very special.

Before any of his grandchildren were born, Doc spoke to God and asked him to bless the next generations of his family with unique gifts, powers, and superhuman abilities. He was very detailed in his prayers. He prayed that each one of his grandchildren would be different and that their gift be tailor made in God's image. After his conversation with God, Doc meditated to allow the spirit to speak to him. Doc felt the energy in his soul that gave him assurance that his prayers were answered.

Doc was in tuned with a higher power and had knowledge of self. Doc did not stop his conversation once he felt it in his soul. That conversation opened the door for a better relationship with God. His faith became impeccable with life's obstacles when he encountered them. Doc spoke to God every day and every chance he had. His life changed from stressed to blessed once his relationship with God became stronger. Doc was not selfish in his prayers. Even when he had an encounter with a racist group that nearly ended his life, he never complained.

On April 3, 1968, Doc was packing his car up to travel to Memphis, Tennessee to join Dr. Martin Luther King Jr. in a peaceful march. Doc was attacked by a group of men that struck him with bats and the butt of a shotgun. He suffered two broken legs that remain lame. Doc was forced to use a walking stick since the attack.

Doc knew that he had to do something to fight the hate and injustice in the world. He did not want his family or any of his loved ones to experience the prejudice and discrimination that he experienced firsthand.

Doc studied the law by reading books and talking to people that he trusted. He also attended several meetings with local civil rights leaders and was very instrumental in the movement.

He passed all his knowledge to his children and friends with the intent to plant the seeds that would blossom a generation built to fight oppression. Doc traveled the country fighting for the cause and helping others in the civil rights movement. He often was from home months at a time. He knew that was the sacrifice he had to make because it was heavy on his heart.

Each grandchild had an interesting relationship with their grandparents Doc and Rosey, due to them basically raising them all. As it was stated earlier, they all stayed with him and Rosey at some point in their life. Doc taught each one of his grandchildren how to move in the world and the importance of finding their self-awareness to allow them to identify their powers and discover their Inner G. Doc didn't know what each grandchild's powers were. He knew they all were gifted but it would be up to them to identify it.

He encouraged them all to read books about their African heritage so they would know where they came from and empower them. He gave them access to his self-made library, requiring them to all read books daily.

Seven, one of the grandson's spent the most time in the library. He was the introvert and one of the first to identify his powers. Doc raised them all to be leaders in their own lane. His grandchildren were the seeds that grew into trees of knowledge, wisdom, and power that would fight oppression, hate, injustice, and all the evils of the world.

Doc presently lives in a three bedroom with his wife Rosey. Rosey stood by Doc through all the obstacles that they faced growing up.

He continued to pray and meditate daily to connect with God. He built a praying room where he spends several hours a day. Praying allowed him to talk to God and meditating allowed God to talk to him. Doc would spend hours meditating. It relaxed him and refreshed his body. Doc taught all the grandchildren to meditate.

"Meditation is when you mute the mind," Doc would often say.

Staxx took a liking to meditation and became very familiar with the mind and how it works. He always believed that meditating helps assuage stress and uncluttered the door to your spirit, creativity, soul, and divine veracity. He really believes that meditation is an innovative way of silencing one's thoughts until it touches the base of the mind.

Chapter 3:

MISS FLO

Years ago.

A chocolate brown 1988 Oldsmobile Cutlass Supreme arrived in the driveway, driven by Mrs. Renty. Rosey opened the passenger side door and stepped out. She was dressed in an all-white housekeeping uniform. The dress stopped slightly below her knees. She wore all-white slip-resistant shoes. Little children ran around the yard playing. She walked up to the front door of the small brick house and waved goodbye to Mrs. Renty. Seven approached his grandmother and assisted her with her bags. The other kids continued to play and run around the house. Egypt and Solei played hopscotch along the side of the house where they had sketched the blocks with a stick in the dirt. Rosey walked in the house and was greeted by one of her oldest granddaughters who stayed with her. The house was clean and warm.

"Hello Grandma," Kenya said.

"Hey baby, you sholl got it clean in here," Rosey said. "Seven, put that bag in my room by the window."

Seven took the large grocery bag and did as he was told: he placed it in the room next to the window. He walked back out to the front room and noticed his grandmother was tired. He went to the record player and pulled out an album with a white cover. On the front was a handsome black man sitting in a white wicker peacock chair with his right leg crossed over his left leg. The man had an afro, and his smile, which showed his white teeth, was pleasant. Two green plants graced the white background, a potted fern hung from a hook and the other in the threshold. Gold rings and bracelets complemented his ivory-color suit. His platform shoes were off-white and complemented his black dress socks. Seven removed the vinyl from the record sleeve and placed it on the platter. Subtle crackling sounds emerged once the needle touched the vinyl—then the sounds of a soothing acoustic guitar with a slow-tempo drum. Rosey, who had started preparing supper, looked up and smiled. She retrieved a Mason jar of fresh tomatoes and okra from the shelf above the stove. She slightly patted the bottom of the jar to loosen the top and then turned the top counterclockwise until she heard the refined pop. Rosey then turned the knob on the gas stove and listened, for a moment, to the ticking sound of the stove being ignited. A blue flame appeared on the eye as she turned the burner on low. She looked at her hand and saw years of laboring, cleaning, cooking, consoling, fostering, and love. Fifteen seconds into the song, a soulful voice serenaded her as she boiled a pot of rice. Rosey sang along as she opened the kitchen window.

Her grandkids began to flock to the back door as soon as they smelled the fresh okra and tomato soup simmering. Thirty minutes had passed since she had arrived, and already Rosey had prepared supper for the entire family after a twelve-hour shift on Hilton Head. Her family called her Rosey because of her father, who had given her that nickname because of her big red cheeks. Everyone else referred to her as Miss Flo.

Supper was ready, and she served each bowl of soup. The pot that she dipped the soup out of was steel, tall, and deep. The steam from the pot was like a beacon. Kenya was the first to get a bowl because the family viewed her as Rosey's favorite grandchild. Rosey never showed favoritism though. If you were alone with her, she would shower you with words of affirmation that made you feel like the most special person in the world. Rosey sat in her favorite chair and watched her grandchildren eat. She smiled and eventually fell asleep. Kenya made sure all the dishes were washed once everyone was done. Rosey woke up from her nap and went to her bedroom. She opened the bag and dipped a cup of bird food out of it. She then sat and waited patiently. She longed for God's messengers to stop by her window as they did when she was a child. Moments later, Doc entered the room and hugged her from behind and thanked her for keeping his food in the microwave with a cover over it. That took Rosey's mind off the birds not arriving. Doc left the room and went to eat and read.

The next morning, Rosey got up and made breakfast for the family. Brix, who was a heavy sleeper, was suddenly awakened by the boiling sound of grits bubbling and scrambled eggs sizzling on the stove. The enchanting smell of breakfast sausage grease lured him out of his warm bed. Doc sat at the table drinking a cup of coffee and discussing his plans for the day with Rosey.

"Don't forget to take that package to Lijah. I called Maggie to let her know that you'd be dropping it off. Be careful. It's supposed to rain later, and you know you can't drive too good in the rain."

Chapter 4:

BOOK OF BRIX

The upbeat tune of "Black Spasmodic" by A Tribe Called Quest pulsed through the black pickup truck.

Brix, the owner of Doc's Barbershop, turned down the volume and pressed the Bluetooth speaker button to call Fadez. The phone started to ring.

Fadez picked up and answered, "Doc's Barbershop!"

"Nephew! What's good?" Brix replied.

"I'm good, Unc! Are you coming through?" Fadez asked.

"Yeah, I'm on my way. Do you need anything?" Brix asked.

"Please grab me some lunch. I'm starving!" Fadez answered.

After the call Brix stopped at a pizza joint that was en route to the barbershop. He ordered five large pizzas to go. When he arrived at his shop, he grabbed the pizzas in one hand and opened the door with the other.

As he walked in the door, he announced jokingly, "Brix's pizzas! If you enjoy life, don't touch my slice!"

The customers who knew him started laughing and shaking their heads. Others looked on in confusion. That was Brix.

He was 6'8", 230 pounds of muscle, and full of humor. When asked why he laughed so much, his signature reply was "If you knew what I knew, you would know that laughter keeps me from crying." Brix was a giver too. Even though he ate one box by himself, he bought pizza for the entire shop. Brix was the life of the party whom everyone loved being around.

He walked around the shop and greeted everyone with a pound. The kids who were in the shop looked at Brix in astonishment. His stature reminded them of LeBron James.

Brix gave the four boxes of pizza to Shag T., one of the barbers. Shag placed them on a table for everyone to help themselves. Brix went over to Fadez and dapped him up. They started chopping it up.

"Is Diane working today?" Brix asked.

"Yeah. Why?" Fadez replied.

"Nephew! Don't be a hater," joked Brix.

Fadez started smiling. "You know it's not in our blood to hate."

As Brix walked in the back to chat with Diane, Fadez was putting the finishing touches on his client's head. Fadez's skills with the clippers were superb. One could say Fadez had remarkable speed that worked well to his advantage.

Those who were waiting sat patiently and looked on as Fadez worked. He didn't rush, not even on the bratty kids who were afraid of getting a haircut. He completed each head with style but extremely fast.

Fadez was only nineteen years old, but he managed the barbershop and the staff. Fadez was the youngest out of the group; however, his ears were glued to the streets. He spent several hours reading in Doc's library and trained with Uncle Glaze, the Geechee Warrior. Glaze was a supreme warrior and the cousins' uncle.

Brix and Diane started to talk as she retwisted his locks into a style.

"How's it going, D.?" Brix asked.

"I'm good," Diane replied. "Sticks and Stems came back the other day."

Sticks and Stems were two guys who grew up with Fadez. They were well-known troublemakers and stick-up kids.

"They came in early last Tuesday morning around nine thirty. They stayed until around noon and left. The crazy part is, they didn't even get a cut," Diane continued.

"They were scoping out the place, but nephew can't see that," Brix replied.

"Yup, you are right," agreed Diane.

Brix knew Stems and Sticks from other kids and some of their older relatives. He didn't like them, but he kept it cool for the sake of Fadez. Brix told Diane to keep an eye on them and let him know the next time they came back to the shop.

Brix was born in the Bronx when his mother and father moved from South Carolina. Shortly after he was born, they got into a dangerous car accident on the way home from the hospital. Brix's hand was broken, and his bones shattered, and he had to have a major surgery to save it. Metal rods and screws were placed in a few of his tiny fingers. Over time the bones in his hand healed, and the rods and screws miraculously disappeared. The doctors had never seen such a thing. Many X-rays and MRIs were conducted in search of the metal implants, but nothing was ever found.

Brix came to South Carolina when he was around ten years old. He stayed with Doc and Rosey off and on, mostly over the weekends, when his mother went to work. In the library Brix read books that dealt with the future and strength. He took a liking to driving because of Doc teaching him how to drive his pickup truck. Brix became Doc's personal driver, taking him to run errands before he even had a license.

While growing up in New York, Brix soaked up the hip-hop culture. He enjoyed going to the park and witnessing the DJs battle and the B-boys dance to the breakbeats. He was too big to break-dance, but he embraced the emceeing element of the culture.

Brix started having quick flashes of images when he was ten years old, kind of like pieces to a puzzle. He would see things in his mind crystal clear. He thought nothing of it. It began to feel normal to him. Doc told Brix that it was a gift from God, and he gave him more books to read that would allow him to become fully aware of his powers. Brix learned to embrace his powers at an early age.

One rainy night Doc woke Brix up to have him drive him to a friend's house to drop off a package. Brix loved when Doc asked him to drive. He jumped out of his bed and got dressed. Before he ran out of the door, he grabbed his Eric B. & Rakim cassette, *Paid in Full*, a birthday gift from Doc. After Rosey gave Doc a warm kiss, he placed his satchel over his head, with the strap resting on his right shoulder. She also gave Brix two small apples, which she knew her big grandbaby loved. Rosey watched from the front door as the two got into the truck.

Brix pushed his cassette in the deck and put on his seat belt.

"I'm not going to turn it up loud," Brix assured Doc.

Doc looked at Brix and cracked a slight grin. "You took the words right out of my mouth," he replied.

Everything felt familiar to Brix. He couldn't piece the puzzle together in his mind, but he felt strongly about the current situation. While driving, Brix went into a mental flash. The glass from the office window shattered, and pictures fell off the wall. Papers slowly fell like confetti and covered the floor. Bullets entered slowly into a man's flesh. He opened his eyes, breathing heavily, looking at Doc with both hands on the wheel.

"I just had a crazy vision!" Brix yelled.

"Focus on the road, son, and slowdown in this rain," Doc instructed Brix.

Brix sensed that something bad was about to happen. At that moment a larger vehicle doing 80 mph in a 45-mph zone intentionally swerved in their lane. It struck the passenger side of Doc's vehicle, sending the small pickup truck tumbling off the road in a ditch. Brix took both his hands off the steering wheel, unfastened his seat belt, and grabbed Doc, covering him.

Brix was breathing fast and deep, and there was little space available for him to move as he continued to cover Doc. The rain showered on the bent truck as the windshield wipers scraped the window.

Brix asked Doc if he was okay.

Doc replied, "I'm okay, son. How about you?"

Brix had deep gashes all over his body, which revealed his flesh.

"You have to get us out of here," informed Doc.

Brix released Doc and opened his left hand toward the metal door. He felt a power that he had never felt. His left hand started tingling as bending metal screeched, and the door went flying in the air. Brix climbed out of the truck and out of the ditch. He then pointed both his hands down at the crashed truck. Doc felt the truck moving out of the ditch. He looked up and saw Brix grunting with both arms trembling as the vehicle reached level ground. Brix fell to the ground and panted. Doc started praying as Brix lay there in astonishment.

"What just happened?" Brix asked hesitantly. He looked at his hands with confusion on his face. His palms were throbbing. He raised them to a metal pole streetlight. The top of the pole gradually bent into the shape of a cane.

"I don't understand. How did I…" Brix struggled to ask his grandfather.

"Don't question God's gift," Doc said as he began to thank God for revealing Brix's powers.

Brix checked his body for injuries. After checking from head to toe, he discovered cuts and slashes on his upper body and arms. He rushed and pulled Doc out to see if he was injured. Doc immediately directed him to check on the other driver involved in the crash.

Brix ran over to the large pickup truck where a man was trapped inside. He noticed a Confederate flag license plate on the front of the truck. He stretched his open palm to the smashed driver side door. The metal screeched as the door popped off. He saw a helpless white male. He did not have a seat belt on, and it seemed his head had hit the steering wheel. The man's eyes opened, blood covering his face.

"Hold on, I'm going to get you out of here," Brix said.

As Brix leaned in the truck, the man grabbed his wrist and squeezed it tight. He then tried to reach for something. Brix quickly pulled him out of the truck. He noticed the initials "SS" on the hat he wore.

Brix walked back to Doc, keeping his eyes on the mysterious man. Sirens sounded as first responders arrived on the scene. EMS ran directly to the white male as he lay helpless on the wet ground. Minutes passed and several police cars also arrived. EMS loaded the man and Doc on separate stretchers as one officer took a statement from Doc. A detective arrived on the scene and immediately started observing what the other officers missed. He noticed the tire marks where the truck was removed from the ditch. He also noticed that there was not a toll truck around. He looked at the streetlight and noted its odd shape. He looked over at Brix; his sharp stare made Brix feel uncomfortable. He was known around town as the best detective, and his proficiency left no case unsolved. Brix watched him as he pulled on a cigarette, the end blazing a bright orange hue. He approached Brix, took the final pull from his cigarette, and flicked it.

"Det. Ivan Vex," he said, extending his hand.

"Brix," he said while he shook the detective's hand. The metal wire in the investigator's mouth began to shift from side to side.

He pulled his hand from Brix and stared at him, adjusting his jaw with his hand.

"That's a mighty firm grip you have, young man," he said.

"I'm sorry," Brix said, noticing the tattoo on his neck. Two snakes curled to form two *S*'s.

Another officer went to examine the other vehicle. He searched inside and outside. He found a liquor bottle on the floor and a loaded gun with a silencer. The officer also searched the glove department, where he found a patch to a biker's jacket with the initials "SS." The officer looked around cautiously to see if anyone was looking. He also found a file. He placed the patch in his pocket and picked the file and gun and placed them in his jacket. Doc saw every move that the officer made.

Meanwhile Brix was getting irritated as Detective Vex interrogated him. Brix knew that he could not tell the detective that he was driving. Even though he was not at fault, he did not have a license to drive.

Detective Vex questioned Brix about the door being off the trucks. He also advised Brix to come to the station for further questioning. A small lady holding an umbrella approached the scene.

"Brix, don't you get in that car!" the lady yelled.

"Miss Flo, long time," Detective Vex said.

"What are you doing with my grandson?" Rosey asked.

Rosey took care of Ivan years ago. She worked for his parents as a housekeeper. Ivan was not the innocent child who once played with Rosey's boys. He had evolved into a notorious detective who was known for manipulating evidence and witnesses. He openly accepted bribes from local politicians to sway their votes and to start smear campaigns.

"You all right, son? Go in the ambulance with your granddaddy. Look at me! Don't you ever talk to them without a lawyer present," Rosey said.

"Yes, ma'am," Brix said as he hugged her.

"Stay away from my family!" Rosey said as she walked to the ambulance.

Detective Vex tipped his fedora that rested on his shaggy hair. Doc handed the cell phone to the kind EMT worker who allowed him to call his wife. Rosey went to the back of the ambulance to make sure he was well taken care of. Doc nodded, and the ambulance drove off.

When they arrived at the hospital, a group of angry white men were all waiting outside. Doc knew exactly who they were. Several men wore hats with the Confederate flag on them.

Brix asked Doc if it was safe to get out of the ambulance, and Doc told him no. The driver noticed the men and took an alternate entrance so they could enter without being seen. When they entered the hospital, Brix went to a phone and called Doc's lawyer. Doc was well connected in the community and knew several experienced lawyers. Brix told the lawyer that his grandfather was in an accident, and he needed him to come to the hospital immediately. The lawyer told Brix he was on his way and not to talk to anybody until he got there. Brix told Doc what the lawyer said. About thirty minutes passed before the lawyer arrived.

The lawyer was a tall, distinguished old man, dressed in a suit. He came directly to Brix.

"Are you Brix?" he asked.

Brix answered, "Yes, sir, I am. Are you Daniel?"

"Call me Danny," he said as he extended his hand for a handshake.

He then told Brix to come with him as they entered Doc's room. Danny greeted Doc with a hug and asked if he was okay. Doc confirmed that he was fine and began to explain everything that happened, including the part about the officer placing something in his shirt.

Danny started writing down every detail that could play a role in court, just in case. He then told Brix not to worry about anything and thanked him for taking care of Doc.

This event stuck with Brix, and he would always remember it. From that day Brix knew his grandfather would be there for him, and he would do the same for his family. This event took place when Brix was around thirteen years old, and since then he and Danny became close. Danny taught Brix law and how to start a business.

Back at the shop, Fadez saw Brix and Diane talking in the back. He knew Brix had a thing for Diane, but he didn't know Diane was keeping an eye out for Brix and funny activity such as screened numbers calling the shop after hours. Brix, his brother Blaze, and Fadez all moved to Atlanta after they moved from Beaufort, South Carolina.

Brix knew he had to watch out for Fadez because he was young. Although Fadez felt he could take care of himself, Brix kept Fadez grounded and on track; well, at least that was what he tried to do. Fadez was not the type of guy who could be kept tied down. He was young, handsome, and successful and not ashamed to let people know it.

The two would always have long debates about music. Brix was a New Yorker, so he bled '90s hip-hop. Fadez loved Trap music. Every morning when he opened the shop, he would have Future blasting throughout Doc's Barbershop.

Fadez was very responsible when it came to handling business in the shop and regarding his family. He knew that family was important, thanks to Doc teaching him this at an early age.

Chapter 5:

BOOK OF FADEZ

Fadez would spend weekends with Doc and always had the most interesting questions to ask him. Doc would answer each question and suggest books for him to read. Fadez felt like he didn't need school because it was a waste of time.

Fadez first became aware of his powers in elementary school. He would always finish his work first. He often felt odd that he didn't take as long as everyone else. He was also the fastest in sports amongst the other kids, literally finishing first in everything. Fadez would get bored in class due to the work not being challenging. Combined with him always finishing before everyone, he became a class clown. He spent several hours in detention, but because he was always bored, he continued to disrupt others there as well.

One day Fadez got suspended from school for getting into a fight and Doc had to pick him up. During the ride home, Doc had a long discussion with Fadez about his ability and lack of interest in attending school. Doc taught him how to embrace his speed. Fadez described it as feeling as if the world was slow motion and he was moving at a normal pace.

Doc told Fadez that he was a barber once and offered to teach him. Fadez was very excited about learning how to cut hair. When they got home, Doc sent Fadez into his attic to retrieve a briefcase. In the briefcase was a set of clippers, safety razors, and other barber equipment. It had been decades since Doc last used the clippers. He sat down with Fadez and taught him everything he knew about barbering. Fadez soaked up the knowledge and hungered to learn more.

Every day after school Fadez would go to Doc's house to learn more about cutting hair, including taking books from Doc's library about barbering. He made sure to read each one. He even started taking the books to school with him and quietly read them after he finished his work. The teachers were relieved that he was reading quietly and not disturbing others. One teacher saw Fadez's interest and hooked him up with a local barber to work in his shop under one condition—he would have to change his behavior in school. Fadez agreed and started working as a sweeper.

Fadez was excited about his new love for barbering and became extremely passionate about the craft. He would spend hours learning from the barbers in the shop. One day at his grandparents' home, Fadez was practicing with a straight razor to get a sharp edge line. As he was lining himself up, he took his eyes off the mirror for a quick second and accidentally cut his forehead. Blood started dripping down his face as he panicked. Fadez dropped everything in the sink and searched for a towel. Suddenly the pain rapidly vanished. Fadez wiped the blood from his face and looked in the mirror. There was not a visible cut or sign of a cut, except for the blood.

Fadez was at a loss for words. He thought he was tripping out, even hallucinating. He picked up the razor and gently slid it across his opened hand. As his flesh opened, blood oozed out. Then his flesh closed back up as if someone pressed rewind.

Fadez tried it again, this time on his face. Again, his flesh opened and then closed on its own. Fadez called Doc into the bathroom and demonstrated his newfound power. When Fadez took the razor and sliced open his arm, Doc screamed.

"What are you doing?" Doc asked with concern in his voice.

Fadez quickly responded, "Wait, Granddad. Look at this!"

Fadez's flesh healed within seconds. Doc knew it was God that blessed Fadez with the ability to heal at a rapid pace. Doc then explained to Fadez that God blessed him with the powers of supernatural speed and healing.

"I think it's time you go with your Uncle Glaze and practice," explained Doc.

Fadez and Uncle Glaze didn't get along. He had noticed that all his older cousins spent time with Glaze and became nice with their hands. Fadez was up for the challenge, but he was not ready for Uncle Glaze.

Fadez trained with Uncle Glaze along with Dax and Breeze. The training was intense. They focused on agility, strength, speed, and discipline. Fadez struggled with the discipline, but he excelled in the speed training. The guys spent several weekends training with Glaze.

Back at the shop, Brix and Fadez started closing. Fadez usually closed the shop around this time, 8:00 pm, to make sure he wasn't in the shop alone for too long.

"What's good with Sticks and Stems?" Brix asked Fadez as he swept the cut hair on the floor.

"They're good, I guess. Why do you ask?"

"I haven't seen them in a while."

"They usually drop in and out from time to time."

"Just watch those dudes around the shop," Brix warned. "Anytime someone comes around to just chill and don't get a cut, they have intentions. Especially those two clowns. I know you grew up with them and all, but those dudes are grimy, remember they were the two that broke into Staxx's home when he was away and stole his jewelry."

"So, Diane told you they were in here just chilling?" Fadez asked with a look of unbelief on his face. "Wow!"

"It doesn't matter who told me they were here; I'm just letting you know that you need to keep an eye on those guys. You know and I know that they are stick-up kids! Just be safe," barked Brix.

Fadez didn't like the fact that Diane was reporting what went on in the shop. He knew deep down inside Brix was right, but it was his ego that got in the way.

"So, you think I can't run the shop or something?" Fadez said, irritated.

"Let's wrap it up here. I need to get home, because obviously that entire conversation went over your head." Brix said.

Fadez took half of his earnings and placed it in the safe in the back room where he kept money in the shop for emergency purposes.

Brix, Diane, and Fadez were the only three who knew the commination to the safe. While Fadez was putting away the money, Brix started wiping down the barber chairs.

In the shop, there were four barber chairs aligned precisely. Diane's location was in a separate room where she conducted her business.

The phone rang and Fadez yelled out "Yo, get that!"

"Who is this calling after hours?" Brix thought. "Yo," he answered.

The person on the other line hung up once they heard Brix's voice. Fadez came walking out of the back room with a concerned look on his face.

"Who was that?" he asked.

"I don't know. They hung up," answered Brix.

"Good!" Fadez answered in relief. "I'm tired and I don't feel like cutting any more heads tonight."

Fadez walked off to go to the restroom before he and Brix headed out. Brix paused. He heard men outside arguing. He looked back to see if Fadez was still there. He heard the water running in the bathroom, so he knew it was not him. He placed the towel on the counter and walked slowly to the door.

This was the same feeling Brix felt when the drunk driver crashed into him and Doc when he was a kid. He sensed danger!

The men's arguing escalated as he got closer to the door. Brix looked back again at Fadez as he came out of the bathroom to see if he was aware of what was going on. Fadez had no clue as he walked next to Brix.

"Turn off the lights!" Brix ordered in a whispering voice.

Fadez turned off the lights and tuned into the noise outside the shop door.

"Who's that outside?" Fadez whispered.

"Shhh!!" Brix said.

He began to walk slowly to the window. He wanted to peep through the blinds and get a look at what was going on.

The feeling of danger intensified the closer he got. When he raised the blinds, he saw three guys outside arguing. They were about fifteen feet from the door. He couldn't make out who they were because it was too dark outside.

Fadez stood there impatiently waiting for something to pop-off.

"Yo, what are you waiting for? Let's go out and see what's good," Fadez said.

"Shhh! I said wait a minute," Brix replied through his teeth, as he struggled to figure out who the men were and what they were arguing about.

He moved from the window and unlocked the door. Fadez had a look on his face that displayed readiness and concern. Brix looked at Fadez and began to share his plan.

"When I open the door, I want you to close it quickly and lock it," Brix explained with his eyes stretched wide open. He turned the knock knob up then slowly turned the door handle while pulling it opened. The men had started fighting. Brix was at a loss for words when he realized that one of the guys in the fight was Blaze.

Chapter 6:

BOOK OF BLAZE

Years ago.

Thunder and lightning rumbled and flashed outside, making it almost impossible to hear the TV. This was a time, as the elders used to say, to be still.

Whenever the weather was bad, the elders also made sure that all of the electronics were off in the house. They believed that a storm was God doing his work. They would tell you to put a shirt on if you were a boy.

In the house were Blaze, Staxx, Myles, Doc, and Rosey. *Rap City* was on, and the guys were winding down for bed.

"Turn that box off! I'll chop the blood out of you if my name isn't Rosey," said their grandmother from two rooms down.

The guys laughed because they had never heard a phrase like "I'll chop the blood out of you" before.

Doc came in the room and told the guys to turn the TV off while the weather was acting up. Blaze said he would. When Doc left the room, Method Man *Bring The Pain* video came on.

Blaze was a huge Method Man fan. He turned the volume up and started reciting the lyrics in front of the TV, moving his rapper hands like Meth. Staxx and Myles shook their heads and laid down.

"I'll turn it off after this video," Blaze said to Myles.

Blaze was a rebel. He knew he should have turned the TV off as his grandparents told him, but he was stubborn.

The rain poured down harder, the thunder became louder, and the lightning illuminated the room from the window. The guys heard the back door open and close. They didn't know what it was. Staxx got out of bed and went to the window.

"Is someone out there?" Myles asked.

"Yeah, it's Doc outside with a flashlight," Staxx answered.

The screen on the TV turned into black and white static. Myles and Staxx laughed, but Blaze didn't find it funny. He turned the channel to see if the other channels were working. He went to the window and saw Doc walking to the back door.

Blaze lifted up the window and started to climb out of it.

"Man, it's raining out there! What's your problem?" snapped Myles.

Blaze cut his eyes at Myles and then put his finger over his mouth, signaling Myles to be quiet.

"Hush up, I'm going to connect the cable up so I can finish watching *Rap City*."

Blaze jumped out of the window, shirtless into the rainy weather. He saw where Doc had disconnected the wires, so he connected them back. Blaze looked up at the window and saw flashes of light from the TV coming back on.

STTTRRRRRRR BOOM!

Out of nowhere Blaze was struck by lightning. The impact lifted Blaze off his feet and threw him clear across the yard against a large oak tree. His wet body slid off the tree and onto the ground. Leaves and rain showered down from the tree onto Blaze's body.

Blaze lay helpless on the ground. His eyes closed and everything became black. Blaze was unable to move, but he was conscious and aware of what was happening. Then he began to see a bright white light.

Staxx and Myles jumped out of the window and rushed to his aid. When they got to him, Myles started to shake him.

"Blaze, wake up!" Myles cried.

Blaze laid there, unable to move. Staxx placed his hand on his temple and tried to read Blaze's thoughts, but a stronger force was blocking him. He tried again and again.

Suddenly, they heard a voice:

Be still my sons.

Staxx stopped and pulled Myles away from Blaze's body. They looked around to see where the voice had come from. No one was outside except for them. Blaze was totally alert and attentive when the same voice that spoke to Myles and Staxx said directly to him: *You have disobeyed me. Listen to your grandfather and follow his lead. The same power that I brought you down with is the same power I will bless you with. You have a huge task ahead of you. As does your family. Notice all the signs that I have placed in your path; they will help you along the way. Embrace your gifts and powers. You are a supreme being.*

Blaze's eyes opened wide, and he gasped for air. Doc, Myles, and Staxx were there by his side.

He looked at his grandfather and whispered, "I'm sorry."

The current from the lightning flowed through Blaze's body. Doc told Staxx to get the door while he and Myles carried Blaze back in the house. When they got inside, Rosey wrapped a towel around him and helped him to the couch.

Myles and Staxx did not hear the conversation that God and Blaze had shared. Blaze, with a face full of tears, told Doc that God had spoken to him. He told him everything that God had said.

"God said that he had blessed me with power—the same power he used to bring me down with," Blaze shared while crying and sniffling.

Blaze looked at his body and felt the electric current flowing through it. He lifted his left hand and made a fist. He squeezed his fingers tighter and tighter and sensed the electricity gaining momentum. The lights in the house started to flicker on and off. Blaze did the same with his right hand. He made another fist. As the voltage increased in energy, Blaze felt like he was in control.

He closed his eyes and concentrated deeply on the words God had said to him.

Embrace your gifts and powers.

Blaze pounded his fists together, and the power in the house went off. Then there was a loud BOOM! The transformer had exploded.

The only light in the house was Blaze's fists, and they illuminated the room. There was a total blackout outside. Blaze stood there with his fists together while the electricity flowed back and forth between them. His eyes were shut tight. He inhaled and exhaled deeply as the others looked on.

Myles and Staxx's eyes were glued on Blaze as he stood like a statue with his shirt off in the middle of the living room. Soothing sounds of crackling electricity flickered and vibrated throughout the house. The lamp on the coffee table fell to the floor. Blaze's breathing became poised, and he opened his eyes.

Back to the present day. "What the..." Fadez yelled.

Brix stood eye to eye with a Glock 9-mm handgun. Fadez saw everything in slow motion as he reacted with his superhuman speed. Fadez pushed Brix out the door to the left. The perpetrator pulled the trigger, and a bullet slowly ejected out of the barrel of the gun. Fadez moved to the side as he watched the bullet pass through his shoulder. Fadez fell to the ground slowly.

Brix jumped up and grabbed the man who had shot Fadez. Brix slammed the guy against his truck, causing the truck's alarm to go off. The other guy swung at Blaze. Blaze weaved from the punch and countered with a left hook to the ribs that left the guy in a paralyzing shock from the voltage of his fist.

Brix and Blaze ran to Fadez to help him. They slowly picked him up from the ground. Fadez looked at his shoulder as the bullet wound closed.

The two perpetrators got up and ran away.

"Let's go inside," Brix said.

Once they got inside, Brix locked the door. Blaze looked at Fadez sharply and said, "You owe me a cut!"

Brix and Fadez looked at each other and started laughing.

"Really, Unc?" replied Fadez. "I just got shot in the shoulder and all you can think about is a cut?"

"What happened out there?" Brix asked Blaze.

"I don't know bro," Blaze began to explain. "I pulled up and noticed two guys creeping by the shop. When I got closer, they started walking away. I asked them who they were and what they needed. They seemed confused. Then we started arguing. When I approached them, one of them tried to lay me out, so I had to defend myself. He struggled and tried to go for the burners, but I handled him."

"Did you recognize their voice or face?" Brix asked anxiously.

"Nah, I've never seen them before," answered Blaze.

"Sticks and Stems probably sent them I bet," said Brix.

Fadez didn't say anything as he walked to his station and plugged in his clippers.

"Sticks and Stems?" Blaze asked.

"Yeah! They were around scoping out the place earlier last week," said Brix.

"What's up with that, Fadez?" Blaze said.

"I don't know, man. But I will find out who they were. I'm not going to blame them but if it is them it's going to be some smoke.

Believe that," Fadez finally replied. "How do you want me to cut this?"

Blaze looked at Fadez through the mirror and shook his head. "Just line me up."

Fadez looked at the top of Blaze's head and saw a big bald spot.

"You need to go ahead and let me give you a baldy, Unc! Your head is finished," Fadez said, laughing.

Brix agreed. "Yeah, bro, let it go. Your car ain't got no roof!"

"I tell you what," said Fadez. "Let me cut it bald, and if you don't like it, you can let it grow back."

"Fine, nephew," Blaze said. "Just don't mess me up."

"How am I going to mess up a baldy?" Fadez asked.

"How's the business going, bro?" Brix inquired.

"Business is good," Blaze answered.

Blaze owned a small electrical-wiring business that specialized in homes and small businesses. He even had his own crew.

"I need a break though. I think I'm going to go home for a few days to chill out," Blaze said.

"That's a good idea. We should all go and gather our thoughts. Plus we need to see Doc," Brix said.

"Sounds like a good idea. Just let me know so I can plan," Fadez added.

"There," Fadez said as he brushed the cut hair off Blaze's shoulder. "All done." Fadez handed Blaze a mirror and he began to check out his cut.

Blaze stood up and took another look at his head. "Not bad, nephew. I can get used to this," he said.

"That'll be eight dollars," Fadez said, imitating the old barber Mr. Clarence from *Coming to America*.

Blaze just laughed and pushed Fadez's hand away.

It was about 10 pm and Brix felt an urge to call Doc. He walked off while Blaze and Fadez were talking. He pulled out his phone and placed the call.

The phone rang twice.

"Hello," Dax answered as he picked up the phone.

"What's up, cuz?" Brix said.

"Nothing much, Brix! What's going on with you?" Dax replied.

"I'm cool. Working and that's about all. Is Doc up?" asked Brix.

"Nah, he just went to bed," Dax responded. "Do you want me to wake him up?"

"No, don't wake him. I will call him in the morning," said Brix with disappointment in his voice.

"So, how's everything going back home?"

"I can't complain, man. It's all right," Dax replied.

Dax and Brix went on to talk for a while; meanwhile, Blaze had a heart to heart with Fadez.

"I want you to be careful around here, nephew. What happened tonight could have been fatal. Watch what you say around people and especially around Sticks and Stems," warned Blaze. "I knew you grew up with them and I'm not saying it was them who tried us tonight, but you just have to watch how you move around here. Remember this is not our home—we're visitors. You feel me?"

Fadez shook his head in agreement. "You're right. I'll watch what I say and do from here on out," assured Fadez.

"Going home for a few days will be a good idea. Diane can run the shop while I'm gone."

"Yo, Brix! Who you talking to?" Fadez asked.

"This is Dax!" Brix yelled back.

"Tell Dax we're coming home in a few days, so get it ready," joked Fadez.

"When was the last time you talked to Myles?" Blaze asked Fadez.

"If you joined the group text you wouldn't have to ask those type of questions. You can

keep in touch with all the fellas on your own," Fadez said sarcastically. "I'm going to add you to the list now."

Fadez pulled out his phone and proceeded to added Blaze to the group text.

"How's the garden going?" Brix asked Dax.

"It's flourishing plentiful," answered Dax with a light laugh. "I have all kind of

vegetables and fruits in there. When you come down you can get what you want."

"Okay, cool! Let Granddaddy know that I called him and that I will see him in a few days," said Brix.

Brix, Blaze, and Fadez hung around the shop that night talking about what they

could do better to improve business and other joint ventures they could explore. They also planned their trip home.

"We should send a group message to the other fellas to see if they want to come home this weekend, too," Brix suggested.

Group Text: Tuesday

Brix: I know it's late fellas, but I need to talk to you about a couple of things. First, to make a long story short, I'm at the shop with Blaze and Fadez. While we were closing, somebody tried to finesse us, but we handled them, and we are okay. Second, I just got off the phone with Dax and we talked about coming home for the weekend. Just to get away and catch up. We need to see the family. Me, Blaze, and Fadez are heading out Friday morning. I know this is short notice but if any of you can make it home this weekend, it would be good to see everyone.

Myles: Are you guys straight?! I will leave from Charlotte Friday.

Staxx: Be safe out there, brothers! I have a session at 1:00 pm on Friday. Myles, if you don't mind waiting for me, we can leave together.

Myles: That'll work.

Que: Do y'all know who they were? I'll try to make it, fellas. Most definitely.

Breeze: Probably Stick and Stems! I'll be home, fellas! I need to get away from Cali for a while. I'll be there Thursday as a matter of fact.

Seven: I'm in Africa, so I will not make this trip. Are you sure all is well?

Fadez: Yeah, we're good. I got shot in the shoulder, but you know that's a small thing to a giant.

Seven: Still go and get checked out.

Fadez: I'm good, cuz.

Que: Do I need to come to ATL?

Brix: Nah, cuz, we're straight! Just come home this weekend.

Que: Say less.

Night: Be safe out there family. Always read their energy and trust what you feel. I will try to make it down, too.

Brix: I really hope y'all will be able to make it, Night and Que.

Que: I know, cuz. I'll try hard to make it down.

Dax: Granddaddy would be excited to see you all. He talks about you all the time. He always says I pray that you all are using your God-given gifts for the right reasons. It would mean a lot to him to see his grandsons.

Brix: Fadez actually saved my life tonight. One of the guys pulled a gun out on me and I froze.

Myles: Blaze! What up?

Blaze: I'm good, cuz. I hope you are not riding around listening to CDs in that new futuristic whip. Lol.

Myles: I'm glad you guys are okay. Don't worry about my CDs they are going to be worth millions.

Seven: I love y'all! Myles you are the only human that still listen to CDs. Lol.

Fadez: Seven, what are you doing in Africa?

Seven: Believe it or not I'm healing our people and searching for healing herbs. God has placed plants around the world that cure every disease and sickness. We must use our minds and knowledge to find the purpose of each plant and herb. There is a lot of work that needs to be done. I am meeting with someone to discuss future work as well. I will keep you all updated on my journey.

Fadez: Respect.

Brix: I like what you are doing for our people in the motherland. We all need to visit one day.

Seven: That is something I am working on, brothers. Trust the process.

Brix: How's it going in DC, Night and Que?

Que: Running things like usual, cuz. Night on the 1s and 2s of course. Unc with the band.

Breeze: I have a few surprises for all of you. I'll bring them with me.

Dax: I just told Glaze that you all are coming home and he is super hyped. He said you all should have been home because he put diapers on all of you! LOL

Myles: Tell Unc to go wash. LOL

Staxx: You are crazy. LOL

Staxx: For real, fellas, we all are blessed with amazing gifts. If we all come together, I know we can create a force of energy that will change the world. I have dreams of us creating a powerful force.

Dax: There's a lot of stuff going on in the community that needs our attention, too. We can talk when everyone gets here. Granddad is trying to do all he can do. He has the wisdom, but he can really use our energy and strength to help. We must take care of home. The racial tension is in the air. The young are being misled without a leader. You can feel it even more than ever. I'm trying to take care of the family but it's hard. Seeing you guys will mean a lot. We have to take care of our home.

Chapter 7:

BOOK OF DAX

Dax put down his phone and locked the door behind him. He went into the man cave to get some rest. He unlocked the door and placed the keys on a counter.

In the man cave were weapons and tools. On the left wall were antique knives and daggers. Dax's favorite was a dagger that Seven gave to him as a gift from Egypt. Seven made a big deal of the dagger, so Dax kept it close to him. It was gold with a gold scabbard. On the right wall were archery weapons such as a bow and arrows.

Dax was a superb hunter. He lived off the land and grew all his own vegetables and fruits. He practiced a holistic diet and promoted it to his family and friends. Dax didn't care too much for guns, but he was skillful with a bow and arrow. He and his sister ran a farmers market and landscaping business.

Dax and Doc's relationship was the closest out of all the grandchildren. Dax lived about five miles from Doc, but he stayed on the homestead some nights to help with things that needed taking care of. Dax and Uncle Two Thumb built a man cave, which was the fellas' hangout spot when they came home.

When Dax was around twelve years old, he noticed that his body was changing. This change in Dax's body was more mental than physical. He could now predict the weather. He couldn't explain the precognition; he just felt enhanced.

He was always a kid who loved the outdoors. He would stay outside and play until his mother and father would have to go and search for him. Being outside made Dax feel free.

Years ago, Doc noticed Dax watching the news and claiming the weatherman was wrong about certain days in the forecast. Doc would always side with Dax when it came to weather predictions. After a while Doc stopped watching the news and relied on Dax for the weather.

Dax would write out the weekly forecast on the refrigerator in Doc's home. Doc knew this was a gift that God blessed Dax with because he was never wrong on any of his weather predictions.

When Dax was in middle school, there was this girl named Shay whom he had strong feelings for. The guys knew Dax had a thing for Shay but couldn't approach her. They would laugh when he walked halfway to her and then quickly turned around.

The school bell rang, and Dax, Fadez, and Breeze all met in the hall before getting on the bus.

"What are you all doing for the rest of the day?" Fadez asked.

"I'm going on the homestead," Breeze said.

"Me too," Dax replied.

"I'm going to the barbershop," shared Fadez.

"Dax, did you give Shay the letter?" Breeze asked.

"Not yet, man. I'm going to do it tomorrow," Dax confirmed.

"He's scared," Fadez said, laughing.

"Man, ain't nobody scared," stressed Dax. "I just have to wait for the right moment."

"Well, you already wasted an entire school year. Tomorrow is the last day of school, so you better bust a move," joked Breeze.

Dax waved off his joking cousins. "Don't worry about me. I got it under control."

Dax wrote Shay a letter expressing his unfathomable feelings for her. He also asked her out in the letter. The plan was to give Shay the letter before she got on the bus. Dax planned early in the month that on the last day of school he was going to shoot his shot. He didn't tell anyone his plan, but he knew he had to do it.

At 2:30 p.m., the principal gave the students a farewell speech over the intercom.

"Have a great summer, and congratulations to all of the eighth-graders that will be transitioning to high school."

Dax was starting to get nervous. He knew that he had to talk to Shay soon because he probably wouldn't see her again until the next school year.

"I want you all to be safe this summer and enjoy your summer break!" finished the principal.

The bell rang. Sounds of cheers and excitement flew throughout the school. Screams of accomplishments and joy bounced off the walls. Locker doors slammed shut one after the other as the students gathered their belongings.

"I got this," Dax said quietly to himself.

He saw Breeze coming down the hall in the midst of all the students. He checked his pocket for the letter, and it wasn't there. Dax panicked.

"Man! I know I just had it," he said to himself as he searched his pockets.

Dax ran back to the classroom and saw the letter under his desk. "Yes," he said.

Dax picked up the letter and ran outside to look for Shay.

"Sorry! Excuse me," he said as he bumped into the other students.

Breeze saw him trying to make his way out of the school, and he yelled, "Hurry up, Dax!"

Dax made his way out to the back of the school where everyone was chatting and saying their goodbyes. Shay's bus was the last in the row of buses. It was impossible for the human eye to see that far; however, Dax saw her, and he immediately started walking her way as she stood talking to her friends.

As Dax got about ten feet away, he noticed that Fadez was talking to her. Dax stopped and just watched.

He heard Fadez say, "I had my eyes on you all year. I noticed you every day and when you come to your uncle's barbershop. I'm saying, I think you're cool. We should exchange numbers to keep in touch over the summer."

As Dax listened, he was in disbelief. Shay looked like she had just won the lottery. By this time Breeze had caught up to Dax and could see what was going on.

Shay's friends were all excited, as they all wanted Fadez to ask them out. Shay told Fadez yes and wrote her number in his hand with a pen. As she was writing the number, Dax balled up the letter in his palm, and tears started flowing down his face.

Dax gazed at Fadez, and it was not an ordinary stare. This was the type of stare that releases water from the eyes.

Dax shut his eyes tight, and that sunny June weather turned into what seemed like a tropical storm. The sky turned gray; the rain poured down heavy as all the kids ran on their buses in a hurry. The wind gained momentum, and the buses began to shift across the parking lot.

As Dax continued to stand there with his eyes closed, the rain showered down heavier mixed with golf-ball-sized hail. Dax opened his hand, and the letter that he wrote was soaking wet. He tore the letter into pieces and released it into the storm.

Buses started to hydroplane across the parking lot until two buses collided. The impact was so hard that it shattered some of the bus windows. Breeze was able to maneuver through the weather and grabbed Dax.

"Cuz! Snap out of it!" Breeze screamed.

Dax opened his eyes and looked around at the storm that he created. Mr. Bennett, an eighth-grade history teacher, looked on while holding on to a light pole.

Dax looked at Breeze and informed him that he was going home. He began to walk in the rain. Breeze just stood there scratching his head.

"What just happened?" Breeze said to himself.

Breeze caught up with Dax and tried to console him, telling him that everything was going to be all right. As Breeze talked to Dax, he became calmer, and his rage slowly diminished. As Dax calmed down, so did the rain.

Breeze tried to lift Dax's spirit. "Man, there are more fish in the sea! You just have to get your rod and go fishing," he joked.

Dax started laughing, and the sun came out. Breeze knew how Dax felt about Shay, and he also knew what Fadez did was wrong. Breeze and Dax confided in each other.

Breeze threw his arm around Dax and said, "Don't even worry about that, cuz. This will be a summer to remember."

During their walk home, Dax was silent.

"Dax, what happened back there?" Breeze questioned.

Dax remained silent.

"Come on, man! I saw what happened with Fadez and Shay, but I'm talking about that storm. I've known you all my life, and you were never wrong about the weather," said Breeze.

Dax laughed at Breeze.

"I'm serious, man. You told me this morning that it was going to be a sunny, beautiful day. I don't recall you mentioning a category one hurricane in the forecast," Breeze joked.

Dax thought about what Breeze said and tried to explain.

"I don't know. It's like when I saw Fadez talking to Shay, a storm started brewing inside of me. It's like the angrier I got, the bigger the storm grew. Like the betrayal I felt for Fadez was creating a storm inside of me. I felt the power, Breeze."

Breeze and Dax continued to walk. Breeze thought about what Dax said, and things started to make sense to him. They walked in silence until they got to the shortcut through the woods. Breeze didn't like walking through the woods during the summer months because he was afraid of snakes. When they approached the woods, Breeze stopped in his tracks.

"Man, come on with your scary self," Dax teased.

"I'm not walking through those woods in all this heat, cuz," Breeze responded.

"It's actually cooler in the woods than walking on this hot, long street," said Dax.

Breeze did not want to walk through the woods, but he knew it would take thirty minutes off their stroll home.

"Just stay close and keep your eyes open and watch where you walk," ordered Breeze.

The two began to walk and started talking.

"So are you going to tell anyone about today?" Breeze asked.

"No," Dax answered.

Breeze shook his head. "You need to talk to someone. What about Doc?"

Dax actually couldn't wait to get home and talk to Doc, but he wasn't going to let Breeze know that.

"I might," Dax replied.

They continued to walk through the woods, and Dax stopped and put his left arm out to stop Breeze from taking another step.

Dax whispered, "Don't move."

Breeze looked ahead, and the biggest snake he had ever seen was less than two feet from them. The snake was curled up in a striking position, ready for them to take another step.

Breeze said in a very frightened tone, "This is why I didn't want to come this way! What are we going to do now?"

Dax continued to look at the snake and said, "Man, that's a copperhead. If he bites us, our mamas might as well call the funeral home."

Dax was not going to turn around and walk back, so they stood there thinking what their next move should be.

What seemed like ten minutes passed, and they heard leaves and twigs being stepped on. They looked, and it was Glaze and Mungo, who looked like they had just finished a carpentry job. Glaze held a pillowcase that he tossed over his shoulder once Breeze made eye contact with it.

"What y'all doing in these woods?" Glaze asked.

Dax started pointing and answered, "There is a snake right in front of us."

Glaze looked around. "Where at?"

As he got closer, the snake became startled and struck at Dax. Mungo grabbed the snake's tail. The snake quickly turned around. Mungo let the snake's tail go and timed its next strike. Glaze backed up while Mungo positioned himself for the strike. The snake's mouth opened wide and struck. Mungo grabbed the snake by its neck and held it up. The snake was about ten feet long and incredibly thick. Glaze stood in front of Dax and Breeze while Mungo held the snake. Dax and Breeze stood frozen as Mungo gained control of the large creature.

The snake wrapped around Mungo's body. Mungo continued to squeeze the snake until venom dripped from its sharp fangs. The venom oozed on Mungo's flesh into an open cut on his wrist. The snake's head slumped as Mungo crushed the bones in its neck.

"No weapon formed against me shall prosper," Mungo whispered to the snake.

Mungo released the snake and felt dizzy. Glaze ran over to him moments before he fell to his knee. The venom was settling inside Mungo's nervous system.

"I'm all right, Glaze, just help me get to the house," Mungo said.

Glaze told the boys to go home while he helped Mungo. Mungo towered over Glaze, which made it difficult for him to bear his weight. Mungo looked at his arm, which began to change colors and swell from the venom. Glaze felt Mungo's weight shifting on him, so he laid him down in the woods. He slapped his face to try to wake him, but Mungo was unresponsive. Glaze looked around to see if anyone was nearby as he went through Mungo's pockets. Glaze retrieved several hundred-dollar bills, which he tossed on the ground. He then turned Mungo on his stomach and reached in his back pants pocket. Glaze found the Mungaro Chisel. He took the money and the chisel and left Mungo in the woods.

"This was one crazy day," said Dax as he let out a deep breath.

"Yeah! I can tell this is going to be an interesting summer," Breeze replied.

As they walked out of the path, they saw the homestead. The homestead was where they lived. Doc made the homestead very comfortable for his family. It had everything anyone needed to survive. Everyone shared their goods and treated each with respect.

Breeze loved the homestead because he loved being around his cousins. He traveled with his family, who were professional athletes, all over the world. He finally felt stable and secure on the homestead.

Doc and Professor Rand were outside talking when the boys walked up. Professor Rand was giving Doc a recap of the lessons that he had gone over with Seven.

"At the rate he's going, he's going to be ready for college-level material. However, he does seem depressed. Have you noticed a change in his daily behavior?" Professor Rand asked.

"He has been a bit down since his sister went off to college," Doc said.

"What school is she attending?" Professor Rand asked.

"She's a freshman at Howard University."

"Maybe we should take a road trip there one weekend. It will also give Seven a chance to see opportunities," Professor Rand suggested.

"Hey, Granddaddy. Hello, Professor," the boys said together.

"How y'all doing today?" Doc asked.

"Hello, gentlemen," Professor Rand said.

"Go get something to eat. Rosey cooked."

The boys loved their grandma's cooking. They rushed in the house and washed their hands. Grandma Rosey made them two plates and told them to go into the library with Seven. When they got in the library, Seven was sitting down in a corner. He had three books open and was reading them all at the same time.

"What's up, Five Plus Two?" Breeze said.

Seven laughed. "Nothing much. Just catching up on some reading."

Breeze and Dax sat down at the table and started eating.

"Are you going to tell him?" Breeze asked Dax.

Dax remained silent.

"Tell me what?" inquired Seven.

"Tell him, Dax," Breeze said while nudging Dax.

"I think I have powers," Dax blurted out. "I controlled the weather today."

"I mean, I really think I have superpowers," Dax reiterated.

"Nah!" interrupted Breeze. "Seven, this dude made a mini hurricane happen after school when he saw Fadez talking to Shay. That's the girl Dax been feeling all school year. I mean, the wind was blowing like crazy, the rain was coming down so hard it was hurting my face, and dark clouds were everywhere. He just stood there with his hands balled up while all of this is happening, and the weather didn't let up until he snapped out of it."

Seven looked at Dax in astonishment. "Is this true?"

"Yes, cuz, he isn't lying," Dax said confidently.

"Good," Seven said with relief. "Now you need to figure out your powers, Breeze."

"What do you mean by that?" Breeze looked at Dax, confused.

Seven didn't follow up with a response. He just went back into his corner and continued to read his books.

Dax asked Seven what he was reading, and Seven showed him one of the three books he was reading-*The Human Body and the Universe.*

"Hmm, sounds like some deep stuff to me," said Dax.

Dax didn't spend much time in the library on most days. But on this day, he spent the rest of the evening looking at books with Seven and Breeze. Dax walked toward the corner where Seven was sitting, and a book fell off the shelf—*The Science of Weather.* Dax picked the book and looked at Seven.

"Did the books you're reading just fall off the shelf?" Dax asked.

"No, I actually tripped on them," answered Seven. They both started laughing.

"I don't see what's so funny," Breeze said in an irritated tone.

Knock, knock, knock!

"Yo, open the door," said a voice from behind the wall.

"That's Fadez," said Breeze, looking at Dax. "You good, cuz?" he asked.

"I'm straight. You can let him in," affirmed Dax.

Breeze went to the door and opened it. Fadez walked in and looked at Dax then said "What's up?" to him. Dax just shook his head and walked back to his seat.

"What's wrong with him?" Fadez asked Breeze and Seven.

"I don't know. What's going on, Breeze?" Seven asked.

Fadez didn't wait for an answer. "Anyway, did y'all see what happened after school? That storm that came out of nowhere," Fadez questioned.

Dax exhaled.

No one was talking to Fadez, and he felt the tension in the air. Fadez went to the bookshelf, and he started looking through the books to pick one to read. Seven noticed the ink in Fadez's palm.

"You are too old to be writing on your body," Seven said jokingly.

Breeze looked at Dax out of his peripheral vision. Dax looked at Fadez and waited on his response.

Fadez quickly spit something out. "I didn't write on myself."

"Well, who did?" Seven asked.

Fadez rolled his eyes as though he was bothered by the question. "A friend," he blurted.

By this time Dax was getting really annoyed with Fadez and the energy that he was giving off. So was Breeze.

Dax couldn't take it anymore. "That was really messed up what you did today, Fadez!" he yelled. "I should box you in yo mouth!"

Fadez looked at Dax and started walking toward him.

"Who are you talking to?" he asked as though he was challenging Dax.

Seven looked on in confusion. Breeze looked at Dax and felt his pain.

"Hello? Man, what are you talking about?" Fadez asked.

"You know what I'm talking about," snapped Dax.

Fadez began to laugh at Dax. "I know you are not talking about Shay. Cuz, that girl doesn't want you! She gave me the number!"

Dax stood up and walked to Fadez and got in his face.

Fadez did not back down.

"If you really wanted to talk to her, you wouldn't have waited till the end of the school year," Fadez said.

Dax grabbed Fadez by his shirt with both hands and tossed him on the floor. Fadez gathered himself quickly and attacked Dax with a two-piece to the face. Fadez hit Dax so quick that he was shocked.

Seven looked on, amazed at Fadez's speed. Breeze walked by Seven and pulled him so he could get out their way. Dax and Fadez started fighting. Blow after blow! Punch after punch! Fadez used his speed to counter Dax's hits and grapples. Dax felt the same anger he felt at school brewing inside him.

Fadez started talking and taunting Dax.

"You can't beat me, cuz! Give it up! Shay is my girl now," teased Fadez.

When he said that, Dax moved his hands in a circular motion, and a whirlwind formed, scooping up Fadez and tossing him against the wall. The force snatched the books from the shelves, and the bookcases fell from against the wall. Seven and Breeze held on to the desk's legs for dear life.

"Dax! Stop! Please stop!" Breeze screamed.

Dax was zoned out, but he subconsciously heard Breeze. The diminutive voice echoed in his mind. "Dax, stop! *Daaax! Stooop!*"

His hands fell, and the tornado immediately dissipated to nothing. Fadez fell from the sky and landed awkwardly on his leg. His leg snapped like a broken tree branch. It was badly broken.

"*Awww*, my leg!" screamed Fadez in agony.

Dax looked around at the mess that was in the library. The room was a wreck. He looked over at Seven and Breeze, who were keeping their distance in the event more mayhem was to come.

"I told you," Breeze whispered to Seven.

Seven ran over to Fadez, who was on the floor screaming in pain.

"Don't try to move it," Seven said.

Fadez's leg was snapped in half; the bone poked out of his skin and jeans. Breeze and Dax ran to where Seven and Fadez were and gazed down. Dax started apologizing to Fadez instantly.

"What have I done? I'm sorry, cuz! Call 9-1-1, Breeze," Dax begged.

"No! Don't call! I'll be fine," said Fadez.

Seven looked in Fadez's eyes and saw confidence in what he said. Seven rolled up his sleeves, and a bright golden light traveled from his fingers to his forearms. Their eyes widened as they watched Seven's arms illuminate the room. Fadez scooted back from the fellas with his palms to give himself space. The guys moved slowly toward Fadez and watched. The bone that was sticking out of his flesh slowly started to connect to its other half. Fadez started to feel relief from his leg as he placed his right hand on his thigh. The guys witnessed Fadez's bone finding its way back into his flesh and the wound sealing on its own.

"What in the world is happening around here? I've seen enough for one day!" Breeze screamed out.

Fadez slowly stood up and examined his leg. He then looked up at Breeze, who was staring at him with his mouth wide open.

"You and Seven have some explaining to do," Breeze said.

Fadez remained quiet as Seven slowly rolled down his sleeves, his arms turning back to a bronze hue.

"Well, I guess we need to get this place back in order before Granddad comes in and witness this mess," Seven instructed his cousins.

The guys didn't say anything; they just started cleaning. Breeze stood there confused. Fadez used his speed to do most of the cleaning. Dax and Breeze placed the bookshelves back against the walls while Seven gathered the books up off the floor. While getting the place back together, Dax went over to his backpack and pulled out a CD. He placed it in a CD player and pressed Play. Roy Ayer's

"Everybody Loves the Sunshine" started to play. As they harmonized the song, Breeze came across two books on the floor—*Technology and the Future* and *Life under Water*.

Darkness had fallen, and the atmosphere was mystic and voiceless. The foreboding ambiance admired the moonlight that clashed and shone through the slim branches that hung over rotten tree trunks. Mungo lay stranded in the woods. The nocturnal life began to crawl and nibbled at his flesh. An abyss opened a foot away from Mungo. A large shadow with massive black wings walked out of the portal. The moon beamed on the unnatural existence as it grabbed Mungo's ankle and dragged him into the portal. Mungo was never seen again...

Chapter 8:

BOOK OF BREEZE

The clear water glistened under the sun's rays while the waves sang a peaceful melody to the beach. The breeze moved in harmony to touch every living soul in its breadth. Kendrick Lamar's song *"God"* played in the background.

Breeze relaxed in his beach chair, which was engulfed in sand. Around his neck laid a thin Cuban link chain with a black pendant connected. To the human eye, he looked like a beach bum. No worries, just the sounds of waves roaring to block out the distractions of the world.

He was single and owned a three-story beach house with a luxury electric G-Wagon and a sweet subterranean vault. Breeze had mastered the art of living life to the fullest. He was extremely successful from investing in technology, cryptocurrency, and software. Breeze enrolled in the military after he graduated and served time in the Special Forces. He rarely discussed his experience in the military unless he was asked. Even then, he kept it short. He would always say, "It wasn't for me." After he was discharged, honorably, Breeze settled in California. It was then he learned to live a simple life and do what he wanted to do instead of taking orders from others.

While in the military, Breeze kept contact with Seven and Dax the most. Dax went to school at Allen University, and Seven left to travel the world through a program for gifted teens that was funded by medical researchers. Breeze felt like the military was the best way for him to leave home and see the world. At least that's what the grown folks had always said: "Enroll in the service, see the world, meet new people. Ain't nothing for you here."

Years Prior. A knock at the door woke up every soldier in the room.

BOOM, BOOM, BOOM!

"Get up and get dressed! You have three minutes to meet me at Battleground 537," yelled one of Breeze's commanders.

Breeze jumped out of bed and started to get ready. He placed a book that he was reading under his pillow and continued to get dressed.

Breeze was in a specialized training that was very intense. He had no contact with the outside world so he couldn't reveal the classified information he'd learned. The training consisted of military-technology development. Breeze was amazed at how advanced the government was. He soaked up all the information like a sponge.

The training took place on a remote, clandestine island. Breeze had been handpicked by the CIA as a result of his superior performance. Although Breeze liked all of the training, he didn't like feeling like he lived under a microscope.

The training was supposed to last an entire year. Breeze was physically ready for the training, but he missed his family and having a life. His daily routine was physical training, eating, classes, more classes, and sleep.

During the rare free time he had, Breeze would often walk the island with one of his friends, Lampkin, a young white man from New Jersey. He and Breeze were roommates and became very tight.

"Where do you think we're located?" Breeze asked Lampkin one afternoon.

"I don't know, son. Wherever we are it's nice. You feel me?" Lampkin replied.

"Yeah, you think we made the right decision by coming here?" Breeze asked.

"Remember, son, they chose us," Lampkin said, laughing.

Breeze shook his head and laughed, too.

He walked the island to get familiar with his surroundings because that was something Doc always instilled in him to do. You never know what could happen. Breeze made a map of the island and kept it with him everywhere he went. Lampkin was the only one who knew of this map.

The Island was large, but that didn't stop Breeze from exploring every nook and cranny. One night Breeze couldn't sleep, so he decided to take a walk to ease his mind. He got dressed and headed out. While leaving his building he noticed a light on in one of the other facilities. Breeze walked to the building to see what was going on. As he got closer, the light went off.

Breeze felt something wasn't right. "Who could be up at this time of night?" he thought to himself.

As Breeze got closer to the building, he saw two men in camouflage with assault rifles guarding the door. They spoke with a foreign accent. Breeze went into stealth mode and snuck around the back of the building. Breeze positioned himself to look through the window and saw an interrogation taking place.

The person that was being interrogated was one of his instructors. He was tied up to a chair with only his mouth revealed. Breeze couldn't make out what the interrogator was saying, but he knew from his tone that he was trying to get something out of the instructor. Breeze got closer to the window and noticed that there were four men in the room, including his instructor.

"Where is it?" one of the men yelled.

"Just kill me because I will not tell you," the instructor said bravely.

The man drew a machete from his holster and pointed it at the instructor's hand.

"I will chop off your hand in five seconds if you don't tell me!" the man warned. He started to count down. "Five, four, three, two…"

The instructor did not budge when he got to one.

"Stand him up," the man said.

The other men grabbed the instructor and then forced his right hand down on a desk. Without warning the leader swung his machete down and chopped off the instructor's hand. The instructor yelled in torment.

Breeze stepped back from the window as his heart rate increased. He never thought he would be witnessing something like this. The man stooped down to the instructor and whispered something to him. The instructor looked at him and spat in his face. The man laughed and wiped the spit away.

"You are a loyal fool," he said.

The man picked up the blood-stained machete from the floor and gently put it on the back of his neck.

Breeze knew he had to do something. He quickly moved back to the front of the building where the two guards were. The guards were not at the door, but the door was open. Breeze quietly walked in the building to the room where the men were.

Breeze took a deep breath. He kicked the door open, and the instructor pushed the man with the machete while Breeze took on the men. Breeze fought them all and countered their attacks. The lights went out and Breeze got hold of one of the guns. He started shooting and told the instructor to get low.

Breeze grabbed the instructor's arm and placed it around his neck. The instructor directed Breeze to a secret room in the building that had a safe where several files were. The instructor told Breeze the combination, and Breeze took all the files out and placed them in a waterproof pouch.

"What do we do now?" Breeze asked.

"We have to warn the others of this attack. Take this and hide until help comes," replied the instructor.

"What are you going to do?" Breeze questioned.

"I'm going to distract them," said the instructor. "Now go! Get those files into safe hands. Go!" The instructor pressed a button that opened a wall to exit the building.

Breeze left through the secret exit and headed back to his building. He could hear shots being fired in the distance. Breeze ran to avoid the bullets and the men.

"There he goes!" yelled one of the men.

They spotted Breeze and ran after him.

"Kill them all!" charged the leader.

Breeze hid in spots all over the island using the map he had made. He made his way to the island's only swamp, where he waded deep in the murky water until no one could see him.

"He's got to be on this island! Keep searching, and when you find him, kill him," instructed the leader.

Hours passed. Breeze remained calm and poised. He did not want to move because he was afraid the foreign soldiers would notice him. Three hours passed and Breeze gained the confidence to head back to shore.

When he reached the shore and surveyed the island, he noticed the device that the instructor had given him begin to flash red. Breeze walked to his building and turned on the lights inside. All the men were dead. Breeze started to cry as he walked through the dead bodies. He walked over to his room and noticed all of his belongings were gone. Lampkin was the only person missing. The soldiers had executed all of the men.

Breeze opened the pouch and looked at the objects that the instructor had given him. In the pouch were computer files and other devices that were still flashing red.

Breeze went outside once he heard the helicopters. Three choppers had landed on the island, and several armed men ran toward Breeze. They pointed their guns at Breeze and headed in his direction.

"State your name and your assignment," one of the soldiers ordered Breeze.

"He's one of us!" a voice yelled out.

A gentleman approached Breeze holding a device identical to the one the instructor gave Breeze.

"Are you okay, soldier?" the man, who was a general, asked Breeze.

"I'm okay," Breeze said.

Breeze gave the man the black pouch.

"You are a hero," the General commended Breeze. "The mission and location were compromised, but you saved important files that could be dangerous if put into the wrong hands. Get this man some clothes and a blanket."

That was the longest day Breeze had ever experienced. The general and other higher-ups in the military questioned Breeze for about two hours before they headed out on the chopper. Breeze just wanted to go home and away from the military as far as he could.

While on the chopper, Breeze told the general he wanted to be honorably discharged. The general let Breeze know that he would make it his priority to make that happen for him.

Still, the general wanted to know every detail about what Breeze had experienced during the attack. After about thirty minutes of what felt like an interrogation, Breeze started to shut down.

"I'm the victim here," Breeze said.

"My apologies. One more question if you don't mind," the general said.

"Yes, what is it?" Breeze asked.

"How did you manage to hide from the men during the attack?"

Breeze looked outside and could see the island they had just left. He remained quiet. He looked down at the water they were flying over. As the sun's rays sparkled on the waves, Breeze started to relax. He started to gain an understanding of his power. It was then he wanted to return home and tell Doc.

Breeze continued to look at the water, and he felt a peace that he had never felt before. His mind was clear from all the events that had taken place. The water brought peace to his soul. His life events started to unfold and make sense. Breeze thought back to the books that he had read. He thought about his ability to surpass everyone during water boot camp. Everything made sense.

Breeze looked at the water again and smiled. He was ready to embrace his powers.

Breeze checked his pockets and felt a hard object. The general got up out of his seat to go and talk with the pilot. Breeze pulled the object out of his pocket. It appeared to be a black diamond. Breeze examined the stone.

"Where did this come from?" he whispered to himself.

Breeze closed his eyes and began to meditate. He focused on what had happened while he was hiding in the water. His mind became clear. A voice spoke to him:

This is the heart of all water on earth, son. Take it. It will help you in your most challenging times. I have blessed you with dominion over the water. You are one with the ocean. Embrace your gifts.

Breeze opened his eyes and looked around. He heard the main rotor blades as they spiraled around. He also heard the general and the pilot chatting.

"Are you okay back there, soldier?" the general yelled from the cockpit.

"Yes, I'm okay," Breeze answered.

He placed the black diamond back into his pocket.

"Yeah, I'm good," Breeze repeated to himself with a smile.

Present day. Breeze woke up to his phone vibrating with several missed calls. He touched his neck to see if his necklace was there. He looked around and noticed that the sun was setting. He felt God's presence as he witnessed the sun laying out its love on the water that started from the shore and eventually moved to the core of the sun.

The clouds covered the sun as the sun's light faded to allow the moon to take over. Breeze picked up his chair and headed to his house. As he got closer to his house, he typed in a code on his watch that opened a door to the lower level of his place. Breeze walked in the door and entered an elevator.

He looked at his phone. As he scrolled through the missed calls, he noticed that Night had left him a voice mail. He listened and laughed. Night messing around as always.

"I'll call him back," Breeze said to himself.

The elevator stopped and the door opened. Breeze stepped out and walked to a door that required another code. He then took off his necklace, lifted his right arm in the air, and clinced the necklace. A monitor scanned his black diamond and the door opened.

Breeze's basement, what he called the Black Aquatic, was not your typical man cave. It was a high-tech aquarium with walls made of thick, secure glass, and it was surrounded by the ocean on all sides. It had taken him years to design and develop.

Breeze gathered the things that he would need to travel back home. He didn't pack much. Just two duffel bags. He walked to the far end of the basement where he typed in another code on the glass wall. He moved his hands in a motion that gestured parting. Breeze parted the water that was outside of the basement.

He typed in another code on the glass, and a mini submarine appeared and positioned itself against the glass. The glass walls opened adjacent to the submarine side door, and Breeze walked in. Breeze took out his phone and called Night.

Chapter 9:

BOOK OF NIGHT

A mixer laid between two turntables to the left and to the right. Headphones rested securely over his head. The left platter spun clockwise while Night rotated the right platter counterclockwise. "*Love Hate Thing*" by Wale and Sam Dew played while he cut and blended "*Inner City Blues*" by Marvin Gaye. The crowd applauded and danced.

Night played music for the Underground, a hip-hop lounge. Night was the DJ there three nights a week. This spot played the best hip-hop and live go-go music in town. The band was called 1Pull Production, and they rocked to the go-go DC sound. The Underground was owned by Que and Night. The bandleader was the twins' uncle, Conk.

Night wore a black T-shirt, black jeans, and all-black Nike Foams. His dark-tinted shades hid his eyes. That was Night: cool, calm, and collected.

He continued his set—all on vinyl. Every record was placed in alphabetical order so it was easy for him to locate. He played "Mystic Brew" by Ronnie Foster and "Electric Relaxation" by A Tribe Called Quest.

The audience grooved to the set. Some socialized, some danced, and several looked on as he worked.

"Give it up for my brother, Night!" said a voice that came from the right side of the building.

Night turned the volume down.

"I'd like to welcome you all to the Underground! Relax, mingle, and enjoy the good vibes. Spin that, Night!" Que said, turning it over to his brother.

Night then proceeded with his set. He played "Apache" by Incredible Bongo Band and blended that track with Nas' "Made You Look." His set lasted about forty-five minutes and included hits and bangers from old to new school.

While he was finishing up his set, 1Pull Productions began setting up on stage. Conk gave Night a signal from a drum snare that they were ready, and Night transitioned them in.

The band started playing, and Night slowly packed up his things and headed out.

Night walked about a mile away from the club to gather his thoughts. He critiqued himself on his set, on ways he could do better next time. Night was hard on himself because even though to everyone else he had performed well; he knew he could have done better.

Night opened his hands, and in his palms were light blue and purple rays of energy that glowed from both. He moved his hands back and forth, converting the purple energy into a ball of thermal energy.

He heard a heartbeat that sounded familiar. He walked up to an elderly woman that was slumped over with several layers of clothes. She was holding a cup in her hand that read "The Universe Conspires." Night took a $100 bill out of his pocket and placed it in the cup. He then held the lady's hand and transferred the energy to her. The lady looked up with her eyes squinting to recognize the young man that was dressed in black. She smiled as if she knew who he was. The energy that Night transferred to her traveled through her body and occupied her needs. She continued to smile as she touched Night's face with her hands, which were layered with the destitution of the world.

Years ago. This was the big day everyone was talking about; the solar eclipse was scheduled to take place on the East Coast at 2:06 p.m.

"All right, kids. Today is a very special day. Can someone tell me what today is?" asked Ms. Kinney.

"Solar Eclipse Day!" the class yelled out in unison.

"That's right! Today we will witness a full eclipse that will not occur again for many years. Today we will all witness history. Are you excited?" Ms. Kinney asked her class.

"YEEEES!" the class screamed.

Ms. Kinney opened a box filled with special sunglasses.

"Here we have the special sunglasses that will allow us to look up at the sky to safely witness the full solar eclipse," Ms. Kinney explained. "Who can tell me why it is important to wear special sunglasses when looking at the eclipse?"

Several kids in the class raised their hands. "Yes, Amira."

"If you look directly at the Sun without solar eclipse glasses, you can damage your eyes," Amira answered.

"That is correct!" said Ms. Kinney. "I want you all to keep your glasses on throughout the experience today, okay. Looking directly at the Sun is extremely dangerous. I want you all to experience this event, but you must remember to be safe first. You will be directed when it is okay to take off your glasses. And that is only when, class?" Ms. Kinney asked.

"Full totality!" the class said together.

She took one of the pairs of glasses out of the box and placed the glasses on her face.

"Ta-da!" she said with animation.

All the children in the class laughed.

"Who would like to help me pass out the glasses?" Ms. Kinney asked.

"Me! Me! Me!" the class yelled, with hands raising in the air hoping to be chosen.

Night sat in the middle row with a shy innocent look on his face hoping that he didn't get selected.

"How about ... Night!" Ms. Kinney announced. "Night, would you like to assist me with passing out the glasses?"

The other kids' hands went down as Night agreed to help. Night winked at his best friend Isaac as he got up out of his seat and walked to the front of the class.

Ms. Kinney then read the safety pamphlet out loud to the entire class before she passed out the glasses. Once she was done reading, she took half of the pairs and gave Night the box to assist her.

Night passed out the glasses to the left side of the class while Ms. Kinney passed them out to the right side.

"Does everyone have sunglasses?" she asked. "Raise your hand if you have not received one." No one raised their hand.

It was 1:00 p.m., about an hour before the big eclipse. The school was prepared and had the entire front lawn blocked off for the children.

"Teachers, start heading to your designated areas with your class," a voice said over the intercom.

The kids jumped up out of their assigned seats with chatter.

"Settle down, settle down," Ms. Kinney instructed the class. "I will line you up by the quietest row."

Everyone sat back down in their seats with the intentions of getting their row to line up first.

"Row 2, please get up quietly. Push your chairs in and line up," said Ms. Kinney. "Row 4, you all may line up now. Row 3, you all may line up as well."

Row 1 was the last to line up due to a few students talking. "And finally, Row 1 you all may line up now."

Ms. Kinney looked at the clock on the wall: 1:30 p.m. She walked to the front of the line and once again asked if everyone had their eclipse sunglasses. "Yes!" the class replied in unison. She then instructed her class to show her their pairs of glasses before they walked out the door. Everyone did what she asked, and they headed outside.

Ms. Kinney made sure all of the children in her class were well taken care of. She treated each kid as if they were her own. When they arrived outside, she led the kids over to the front lawn. Mr. Ali and his class were already in their assigned areas. He held up a sign and waved for Ms. Kinney to see.

"Okay, class, let's walk over to Mr. Ali," she said, pointing to Mr. Ali holding a sign. The sign read "Ms. Kinney's Class."

The kids ran as fast as they could to Mr. Ali. There were no chairs for the students, just a large open area for them to gather around and witness the amazing event.

Night didn't run. He walked as he thought about spending the summer down south with his cousins.

"I wonder what Dax, Breeze, Seven, and Fadez are doing?" he said quietly to himself. Night looked forward to going to South Carolina for the summer. He and his brother both were ready to go and stay with Doc. Night walked over to Isaac and some other kids from Mr. Ali's class and stood by them.

"What took you so long, man?" Isaac asked.

"Nothing. I was just walking," Night answered.

The principal spoke.

"Teachers, the time is 1:45 p.m. Please make sure all your students are wearing their eclipse glasses," Mr. Wick said. Ms. Kinney and Mr. Ali again checked their students.

Night looked around and looked up at the Sun. He went off into a trance, still wearing his protective sunglasses. He felt an inner peace that sheltered his soul and secured it with compassion. His confidence grew where his feet were planted. His body absorbed the energy that the Sun was releasing.

Night felt a tingling sensation in the middle of his head.

"Ten, nine, eight, seven, six, five…" was all that could be heard as the entire school counted down in anticipation for the awe-inspiring sight.

The count continued and Night's mind cultivated silence. The mental chatter ceased and allowed prospects to blossom and unfold. His intuition dilated, and vision gushed through his hands. He took off his sunglasses and gazed directly at the partial eclipse. The Moon gradually challenged the Sun. Night saw the last bit of sunlight resembling a diamond ring sparkling as the Moon prepared for full totality.

The Sun struggled to shine along the edge of the Moon. Tears and blood radiated from Night's pupil onto his cheeks. The diamond ring distressed into beads as the Sun's light crept through the sunken valleys along the hem of the Moon. Crickets chirped, animals were anxious, and the temperature dropped.

The students and faculty cheered with excitement as they experienced totality. Night wiped away the tears and discharge from his eyes and dropped the sunglasses on the lawn.

His vision was blurred; he blinked nervously in an attempt to clear it. Night began to panic. His heart rate increased as more discharge oozed from his eyes.

"I can't see!" he screamed.

Ms. Kinney heard Night screaming and ran to him. She saw the sunglasses on the lawn. Ms. Kinney grabbed Night and held him in her arms.

"Oh my god! Someone call 911!" Ms. Kinney said, crying out for help. The attention moved from the eclipse to the child that was screaming for help.

"Night, you are going to have to calm down. Can you hear me?" Ms. Kinney said to Night, trying to comfort him.

Night screamed for his brother, who quickly ran over to him once he realized it was his other half that was causing all the commotion. Que and Ms. Kinney held Night. Night saw darkness and heard several hearts pounding, and every blade of grass began to prickle his legs.

"It's going to be all right, Night! What happened to my brother?" Que screamed.

Ms. Adanya, the school's art teacher, walked to where Night was and picked up the glasses off the lawn.

"Let me help," she said. Ms. Adanya placed two fingers in the middle of Night's eyes between his eyebrows and started chanting a mantra. She started speaking in a West African language that calmed Night down.

Night opened his eyes and saw a blur of a crescent emerging on the other side of the Sun from where the diamond ring began.

"Put your glasses back on folks! This is the final stage of the eclipse!" screamed Mr. Wick to the group.

Night felt the same inner peace in his soul as the darkness transitioned into light.

"Put his glasses back on!" commanded Que.

Ms. Adanya continued her chant over Night's body. He felt a sensation between his eyes again.

Night closed his eyes and felt the warm energy from the Sun shining directly down on his body. His vision was dark; however, everything seemed clear around him. He blinked his eyes to try to remove the darkness and was challenged with his other senses heightening.

Ms. Adanya and Night were the only two that felt the energy shining on him.

She looked at Night and then spoke to him. "The universe is conspiring for you."

Night didn't say anything. He just listened to Ms. Adanya and the rhythmic pattern of her heartbeat. She placed the eclipse glasses back over his eyes and slowly helped him up. She touched his face gently and smiled. Night didn't ask any questions because his intuition gave him a feeling that he was protected.

"What just happened?" Que asked.

Night looked at Ms. Adanya with a long pause between his words.

He looked up at the Sun and said to his brother, "I just opened my third eye."

The principal notified Night and Que's parents and told them about the incident. An ambulance transported Night to the nearest hospital, where he laid on the hospital bed in darkness. A strong smell of latex gloves and disinfectant overpowered him. He heard a conversation being held outside of the room as he rested.

"Your son has suffered severe eye damage. Unfortunately, he will never be able to see again," the doctor said.

Night heard the pulsing pattern of his mother's heartbeat increasing, followed by the vibration of the I.V. dripping in the bag. He touched his eyes and felt every thread that intertwined that made the soft bandage. Night equaled the footsteps and heartbeats of each person that walked past his room. He was amazed at how his other senses had strengthened. He heard the tears oozing from his mother's eyes, lingering on her eyelashes, and diving into the soft wool sweater that she wore. He heard a double-heartbeat pattern emerge from his father hugging his mother that sounded like an Art Blakey drum solo. The door opened, and Night smelled the musk of armpits and the raw stench of an adolescent male.

"Are you up?" Que asked.

"Yeah, I can smell you from a mile away," Night said jokingly.

"Shut up. How do you feel?"

"I feel strange, everything is dark, somehow I can hear everything, and I can smell the flowers and open pack of honeybuns that Uncle Conk is bringing," Night said.

"What are you talking about?" Que asked.

The door opened and their mother broke free from their father and stormed to Night. Uncle Conk strolled in with a bouquet of fresh roses in a blue vase; in his other hand was an opened box of individual honeybuns. Que looked at Night and panned to his uncle, befuddled. Que felt a mixture of emotions. He was sad that his brother's sight had been snatched away. He was also confused as to how his brother had prophesized their uncle's arrival.

Chapter 10:

BOOK OF QUE

Que noticed that Night was not at the DJ booth, but his cane leaned against a speaker. He pulled out his cell phone and called him.

"Hey, what's up? You good?" Que asked.

"Yeah, I'm good. I just stepped out to get some fresh air. I'm headed back now," Night informed his brother.

Que felt better hearing his brother's voice and Night confirming that he was okay. Being twins, Que always felt when his brother was distant or in danger. The feeling he felt when he noticed Night left the DJ booth was one based on concern.

Que walked through his club with pride but remained a very humbled being. The brothers inherited the club from their father. They were the two youngest club owners in the city. The lot and land where the club was built was a haven for slaves who escaped from Southern states.

Gust, one of Doc's sons, settled in DC when he left home for college. Gust and his girlfriend had a set of twins while in college, and Doc and Rosey helped raised the twins while Gust was finishing up school. When Gust graduated, he got a job working as an accountant for a successful businessman who taught him the business side of the club. When Slim died, he left the club to Gust. Gust then taught his boys everything he knew about running a business.

This was the busiest night for Gust at the club. Saturday nights were filled with locals and celebrities that who traveled from all over to enjoy and be a part of the most legendary place in the Northeast.

Everyone looked forward to the weekend just to be a part of the scene. Gust stood six feet four inches and was a clean-cut, well-groomed brother. He wore his wedding ring and a very exorbitant timepiece that matched every suit he owned.

Gust taught his boys how the be respectful men and to be proud of their Gullah Geechee culture. He was extremely conscious about ownership and supporting his people. He taught them the basics such as looking a person in the eye when you talk to them, opening doors for elders and ladies, and always giving a firm handshake. Gust called it the Brix handshake.

Que took after Gust with his style and mannerisms. Que loved going to the club on the weekend to observe and watch how his father interacted with the people and handled business.

When Night did attend the club, he would stay around the DJ booth and imitate the DJ's movements with his hands. Night didn't care too much for the business aspect of things.

Que wanted it all. He would go every chance he got. The boys' mother did not want them to be in the club, but because they were with their father, she knew that they were well taken care of.

"Que, tonight I want you to help me out in my office and watch the books," said Gust.

"Yes, sir," Que replied.

"Night, you also. I know you don't like coming to the club, but I want you to learn how things are operated," instructed Gust. Even with Night being blind, his father showed no favoritism.

"Okay, Pops," Night replied without pushback.

Gust would have an intellectual conversation with his boys in the car every time they rode to the club. It was like he saw things happening before they happened.

"It will be very busy tonight, and at times it may feel overwhelming. If you two ever feel like it's too much, I want you to let me know, and we can go outside and get some fresh air together. Gather our thoughts," explained Gust.

"Tonight the place will be pack up with all types of people that are willing to spend money and looking to have a good time," Gust continued.

Night sat in the back with his sunglasses on, with his head leaning on the window, inhaling, and exhaling deeply which allowed him to hear the live action on the streets. Que was attentive to the conversation and soaked up the game.

They arrived at the club three hours early, which gave them enough time to get things in order. Que followed Gust around the club and monitored how he thoroughly inspected each section of the club. The staff started trickling in, and they all seemed to be happy. Gust greeted each one of his staff members personally and gave them the attention they needed and deserved.

Que watched and witnessed his father use empathy and listen to his staff. He took mental notes on how to treat a person. He noticed that his father was liked and very easy to talk to because in every conversation that was held, Gust did most of the listening.

"Que, come here. I want you to meet someone," Gust said as he beckoned for his son.

Que walked over to his dad, who was talking to a man. Que noticed the man around the club the few times he went. He, too, was dressed in a suit and cleaned up well.

"This is one of my sons, Que," introduced Gust.

"Nice to meet you, Que," said the man.

"Que, this is Lenny. Lenny helps out around the club from time to time," explained Gust. He and Lenny went to college together, but Que never heard his dad mention him before.

"Nice to meet you," said Que.

"Where is your brother?" Gust asked.

"He should be over at the DJ booth helping set up," answered Que.

"Go get him for me," said Gust.

Que walked away to go get his brother. The club was huge, and the DJ booth was on a stage that had a built-in platform. Que walked over to the DJ booth and saw Night helping Boogie. Boogie was a friend of the family, Gust's best friend, and the club's DJ. The twins knew Boogie personally.

"What's up, Que?" Boogie said with excitement.

"Nothing much, Boogie, just helping my dad out. Aye. Night. Dad wants you to come over and meet a friend," Que informed his brother.

Night hooked up the last cord to the mixer.

"Who's over there with your pops?" Boogie asked.

"Some guy named Lenny," replied Que.

"Oh okay," Boogie answered in a dry tone.

"Do you know him?" Que asked.

"Yeah, he's a cool dude that comes around every so often," answered Boogie.

"Yo, Night, I'll finish up here. Go holla at your pops, and here, don't forget your cane," Boogie said.

"All right," Night said grudgingly as he took the red-and-white cane, folded it, and placed it on a speaker.

Que and Night left and headed back to where their father was. Gust and Lenny were not in the same spot that Que left them.

"Did you see where my dad go?" Que asked one of the staff members.

"I think he went into his office," said a guy who was setting up some lights.

The twins headed to the office in search of their father. The office was located on the second floor of the club, down a long hall. On the walls in the hall hung pictures of famous people who came to the club. It seemed like everyone's picture was on those two walls.

Que stopped and looked at a picture. It was a picture taken with Doc and Gust. Doc was embracing Gust with his arm around him, while the other guy in the picture posed neutral. Que noticed very fine details within the picture. He noticed that Doc was not smiling, and he had a concerned look on his face.

"Why did you stop?" Night asked, curious.

The office door opened, and Lenny walked out. Night smelled the luxury cologne and heard his heartbeat raising. Gust walked out behind Lenny.

"Lenny, this is my other son, Night," Gust said proudly.

Lenny walked up to Night and shook his hand. Night shook Lenny's hand, he immediately felt that his energy was off. Lenny looked at Night and slowly pulled his hand away. Night smelled the natural ecstatic chemicals, the excessive dopamine that was backed up in Lenny's body. He felt Lenny's body temperature increasing as the sweat oozed out of his pores. Night also felt a high frequency of energy that vibrated.

"Okay, guys, Lenny and I are going to get ready for our guest. You guys can hang out in my office. I'll come back shortly to check on you."

Que and Night went into the office as their father directed them. Once in the office, Night went and sat on the couch. Que went to his father's desk and picked up the phone.

"Who are you calling?" questioned Night.

"Something's not right about that dude," answered Que. He placed the phone on speaker, and it began to ring.

"Hello," a voice on the other end said.

"How's it going, Granddad?" asked Que.

"Hey, son! The old man is trying to make it," Doc replied.

"Cool. How's Grandma?" inquired Que.

"She's doing good, son," answered Doc.

Que could not small talk any longer. "Can I ask you a question?"

"Sure, son. What is it?" Doc replied.

"There's a picture with you and my dad at his club, and in the picture, there is this guy named Lenny. What can you tell me about him?" Que asked.

"Well, son, my spirit never agreed with Mr. Lenny. That picture was from the grand opening of your father's business. I don't know much about Lenny. That day was my first time meeting him. Your father seems to trust him. I'll tell you like I told your father that day I met him. Be safe. How's your brother doing?" he asked.

"He's doing okay," answered Que.

Night jumped up off the chair suddenly.

"Dad!" he screamed. Night ran out of the office, and Que dropped the phone and headed behind him.

"Bro, what's wrong?" Que asked as he caught up with Night.

Night looked at his brother with a look of terror on his face.

"Something is going on downstairs."

They both ran toward the stairs and heard the noise.

"I told you to have my money at 10:00 a.m., Lenny!" a guy yelled from the bottom of the stairs.

Que and Night looked from the second floor and saw that their father and Lenny were surrounded by a group of men. All the staff from the club were lying on the floor.

"We'll get you your money by tonight. Just leave my club in peace," pleaded Gust.

"Oh! You think it's a game?" the guy asked as he pulled out a gun and pointed it at Lenny.

"You can't save him this time, Gust. Now move out my way," the guy demanded.

Gust stood in front of Lenny and pleaded with the guy that he would pay him at 8:00 p.m. While Gust was talking, Lenny slowly reached behind his waist and pulled out a gun.

"Dad!" Que yelled from the stairs.

Gust looked up at his sons, and a shot rang off. He dropped to the floor. The people who were lying on the floor screamed and cried.

Lenny dropped his gun. Boogie stood up slowly, his face covered in tears. The armed man pointed the gun at Boogie.

"Run, twins!" Boogie screamed as he charged at the man.

Another shot went off, piercing through Boogie's chest. Then another and another. Boogie's body dropped.

"There's a safe in the office. The combination is 38-36-10-2. Your money is in there," said Lenny as he paced back and forth, wiping his nose with his thumb.

The twins ran in the office and locked the door. They placed the couch and bookshelves in front of the door to create a barricade.

Que saw that the phone was off the hook.

"Hello! Hello!" he cried out desperately.

"Que," answered Doc.

"Yes, I am here," Que replied.

"What just happened? I heard gunshots and screaming," asked a concerned Doc.

Que was still shook up.

"Lenny shot my dad!" he managed to yell out.

Night went over to the safe and listened closely to each turn of the knob. His auditory senses heightened with each deep breath he took. Night recalled the numbers he heard Lenny tell the men—38-36-10-2.

The handle clicked, and Night opened it up. He felt stacks of money along with folders. He grabbed his backpack and placed everything out of the safe in his backpack.

"Are you and your brother okay?" Doc asked.

"Yes, we're okay, but the men are heading up here," said a frantic Que.

"I need you to get you and your brother out of there safely," instructed Doc. The office door handle turned but didn't open. It turned again but this time was followed by a shoulder thrust.

"Open the door!" a voice yelled from outside of the office.

"They're here," Que informed Doc.

"Is there a window in the office?" Doc asked.

Que looked at the window and told him that there was a window in the office.

"Go out of the window. Now!" ordered Doc.

The guys started kicking the door aggressively.

Que and Night ran to the window, unlocked it, and opened it. Que looked down to see how far they would have to jump.

He then turned to his brother and said, "We can do it!"

The kicks on the door progressed, and the furniture that was in front of the door started shifting forward. The men had managed to knock the hinges off the door. The door was halfway opened, and Lenny started to push the shelf with his right arm.

"Night, look in the desk to see if there are some matches or a lighter," Que instructed his brother.

Night went over to the desk and searched with his hands as his touching ability enhanced. He fumbled through pencils, pens, and paper clips. Night recalled the sound of a wooden tray being lifted when his father would sit at his desk for a smoke break. He felt handles on the sides of a tray inside the desk. He lifted the wooden layer up. The strong smell of a tightly rolled Cuban cigar escaped from the second layer of the desk. Night moved his hand around and felt a soft leather cigar travel case. He felt the letter *G* engraved on the case. He unzipped the case and felt an engraved cutter. Night smelled the liquid from the cigar torch that was tucked tight in the case. He quickly zipped up the case and threw it to Que. Que opened the case and took the small torch out. He pressed down on the pusher, and a small flame emerged.

Que covered the flame with his hand, and it transferred to his palm. Night was elated as he heard the flickering of the torch and the flame igniting.

"How did you do that?" Night asked in amazement.

"I'll explain later. Head out the window. I'll hold them back," Que said.

Night walked to the window; he didn't hear any heartbeats outside the window. He took two deep breaths and exhaled. Night climbed out of the window and jumped down. Que placed the torch in his pocket, and another flame emerged in his left hand. With both hands flaming, thoughts about his father looking at him before Lenny shot him soared through his mind. This annoyance bred the small flames into large luminous combustible infernos. The flames grew until the sprinklers came on. By this time half of Lenny's body was in the office.

Que, unable to control the fire, pushed with all his might and yelled. He released all the negative energy, thoughts, and resentment he had toward Lenny at that moment. The fire illuminated the room in a bright orange flame. The men crashed through the door, knocking the shelf and couch over. Lenny entered first and was greeted with furious flames.

"*Ahhh!*" Lenny screamed as the fire ate at his clothes and settled on his skin. He patted his body to put the fire out, but the flames were too intense to be extinguished by mere pats. Half of Lenny's body caught on fire. The other guys backed out of the office into the hallway. Lenny screamed as the fire continued to rupture through his tailor-made suit and melted and blistered his skin.

Que ran to the window, looked out, and saw Night waiting on him. He jumped down and landed with agility on his feet.

"Let's get out of here," urged Night.

The brothers ran as fast as they could without looking back. When they got about five blocks away from the club, they noticed a large crowd of people looking up at a building. Women were crying, gasping for air, and men were screaming out, hold on. A little girl was hanging on for dear life.

Night looked up and heard the small heartbeats pounding at a rapid pace. He was able to enhance his hearing sense once he blocked out all other distractions. Taking deep breaths in and slowly blowing out allowed his four senses to elevate into hypersensitivity.

"That's about seven levels up."

Que ran to the building, and without hesitation, he hopped over the first balcony and started climbing the building. His confidence grew with the movement of his body. He reached out his hands and jumped to the second balcony; once he got a grip, he pulled himself up. His hands still hot from the fire left marks on the metal rods.

Night listened to the crowd and felt their energy shifting from fear to hope. When Que got to the third balcony, the crowd started cheering and applauding once they noticed how he gracefully scaled from balcony to balcony.

The little girl was crying in fear of falling.

"Mommy! Mommy!" she screamed as she looked down.

Night remembered the large amount of cash he had in his backpack and the guys who were after him. He listened around and noticed that everyone's voices projected vertically; that conveyed they were looking up. Night's radar senses engaged as he heard the heartbeat patterns that expressed revenge. He smelled the smoke and aroma of his father's club in the crowd. Night held his head down and walked to the front of the building and headed up the stairs.

By this time Que was one balcony away from the little girl.

"Hey, no, no, don't look down," Que pleaded. "It's going to be all right, okay?" Que said.

"Okay," the little girl whimpered out while crying.

Que reached out to her with his right arm, grabbed her, and gently threw her back on the balcony. He pulled himself up on the balcony and took the little girl inside through a sliding door. The crowd cheered with excitement and whistled.

Que looked around in the apartment.

"What happened in here?" he asked.

The little girl, still shaken didn't answer. She just sniffed and wiped the tears from her eyes. The room was a wreck; clothes were thrown across the floor. Roaches raced up the wall where food had hardened.

"Is your mommy or daddy here?" Que asked the little girl.

"I don't know," she said softly and slowly.

Que walked through the apartment, hoping to find someone. The little girl held his hand and walked with him.

"Hello! Is anyone here?" he yelled out while walking through the messy apartment. They walked in a bedroom that had an awful smell. The little girl pulled away from Que and ran to a small mattress that was on the floor. She picked a small bear with a matching winter hat and scarf and held it.

"Who's this?" asked Que, sensing something was wrong.

"He's Saint Jude," the little girl answered.

Que opened the apartment front door and headed out. He saw Night bent over with his hands on his knees, panting heavily from running up seven flights of stairs.

"Is she okay?" Night asked.

"Yeah, I think she'll be all right. Are you okay?" Que replied.

"We gotta get out of here," warned Night. "The men from the club are in the crowd."

Que bent down to get eye level with the little girl. He smiled at her.

"You're going to be okay," he assured her.

The little girl nodded and smiled.

"I'm going to walk with you to the elevator, and I want you to get off on floor number one. Once the door opens, go to the front desk, and tell the person at the desk that you are the little girl that was out on the balcony," Que instructed the little girl.

Que walked over to the elevator and pressed the button for the door to open. He walked the little girl on the elevator and pressed the lobby button. He stepped back.

The little girl looked at him and said, "Thank you."

Que smiled and asked her, "What's your name?"

As the elevator door closed, the little girl responded, "Lauryn."

Que walked outside and saw Night talking on the phone, walking toward the club.

"I'll see you Friday. Drive safe," Night said as he ended his call.

"Is everything okay?" Que asked Night.

"Yes, everything is cool, bro," Night answered.

"That was Breeze. He's headed home."

"Cool! Let's finish up," said Que.

Night looked up at the moon and took off his eclipse sunglasses. He reflected under the moonlight. Everything became silent as he listened for wisdom.

Que looked on as his brother meditated deeply. He did not interrupt him. He felt Night's energy. Night listened closely for whispers. Suddenly a voice whispered subtly, "Go to South Carolina now."

Night blinked his eyes and felt the moonlight coinciding with the essence of light from the message.

"We need to leave tonight," Night shared with his brother.

"Why?" Que asked.

"I don't know. I just feel that we need to go tonight," said Night firmly.

"Well, let me let Uncle Conk know so he can close up the club," Que said.

Afterward they left the club and drove to the airport and took a flight to Beaufort, South Carolina. They both were quiet on the plane.

"What are you thinking about?" Que asked Night.

"Nothing," answered Night.

Que gazed out the window, down at the lights that they flew above.

"Have you ever thought that we should be doing more with our gifts? I mean, it's a reason why I'm able to connect with the sun, moon, and stars, transfer energy…I mean, what is our purpose?" Night inquired.

Que slowly exhaled. "That's been on my mind heavy lately," he responded. "Remember when our house caught on fire?" Que asked Night.

"Yeah…that was scary," Night confirmed.

"It was my fault. I found one of dad's cigar lighters and started playing with it. I was drawn to the flame. I began to light a paper and watched how fast it caught on fire and burned into ashes. I couldn't stop, and by the time I heard Dad and Mom screaming, the entire room was on fire."

"Que! Night! Lord, no! God, please help us! Baby, take Night out! I have to find Que!" Gust instructed his wife.

The fire escalated and spread through the entire house. Gust, choking and coughing from the smoke, felt that he was failing as a dad as he searched for his son. His vision became blurred as dark smoke clouded his view. He fell to his knees coughing. Gust's body collapsed on the fevered floor as he felt the heat from the flames.

Que was crying in the guest room and heard a voice talk to him.

You have used your gift unwisely. Learn to use your gift wisely. I will always be here to guide you. Remain calm in the midst of confusion and have faith.

Que heard footsteps and crackling from the walls being burned. The roof started collapsing as the fire made its way to the top of the house.

A fireman saw Que in the corner and picked him up. He was shocked that he was alive and breathing.

"You're a miracle! I'm going to get you out of here, little buddy," the fireman said.

The fireman dispatched his crew to let them know that he had found Que. As they made their way out of the house, Que looked at the fire as it burned all his parents' memories. The fireman went through a fragile wall that led to his parents' bedroom. The fire had gained full momentum, and the house started collapsing.

The fireman picked up his pace and headed out of the room. Que stretched his arm out and grabbed an item off the burning dresser. The other firemen met Que and his rescuer and led them out of the house. Que looked around, and the entire neighborhood was outside. The feeling was overwhelming as his mother, Grace, came running to him.

"Are you okay?" his mother asked, hugging him close to her. "Baby I thought I'd lost you! Thank you, Lord!" Grace shouted.

She took him over to the ambulance where his father was receiving oxygen. Gust saw his son, and tears of faith and joy slowly trickled down his face. Gust hugged his sons while lying on the stretcher.

Que opened his hand and gave his dad what he had grabbed from the dresser. Gust looked at what Que had placed in his palm and closed his hand tight. He inhaled a deep breath and closed his eyes until wrinkles formed on the corner of his eyes. Grace looked on too and placed her hand over her husband's fist and hugged her family.

"Thank you, God," she said.

Night looked at Que as he finished the story.

"So you too have heard God's voice?" Night asked.

Que nodded in agreement.

"Yeah, bro. I hear his voice all the time during meditation," Que replied.

"He will lead us in the right direction. We just have to trust him and not ignore the signs."

Group Text: Thursday Morning

Breeze: I just made it to the Broad River Bridge.

Dax: I don't see you. I'm on the pier fishing.

Breeze: Which side of the dock are you on?

Dax: The left.

Breeze: I'm about to pull up.

Que: We should be landing in Hilton Head in about an hour.

Dax: This dude just pulled up in a submarine.

Que: LOL. Breeze you a bad boy! Do you have room for me and my brother?

Staxx: LOL!!

Breeze: I got you. Dax and I will come to the Hilton Head beach.

Myles: Yo! I'm packing now. I'll see y'all tomorrow.

Brix: What up fellas! Y'all made it home faster than I expected.

Fadez: LMAO!! That's what's up fellas.

Seven: LOL @ Dax!!

Blaze: Dax?? Fish and grits on you?

Fadez: Yeah Right! @ Blaze

Dax: @ Blaze I got you cuz. @ Fadez whatever lol.

Night: LOL!!

Night: Breeze, we just landed, headed to the beach scoop us from the dock.

Breeze: Dax and I are on our way.

Staxx: Myles when are you coming through??

Myles: I'm coming over tonight so we can leave tomorrow.

Chapter 11:

BOOK OF MYLES

Myles rushed into the class. He looked at his watch and it was 7:45 am. He was late, again.

"Good morning class! Please excuse me for being late. I guess I really need to set my alarm for 6 am. So, I hope you all have completed your assignments because today, we have a pop quiz," Myles announced to his class.

"Really Mr. Myles?" one of the students asked.

"Yes, really," Myles replied.

"I need you all to be sharp. Steel sharpens steel."

"Yeah, yeah, Mr. Myles. We know," Bren said, interrupting Myles. The class laughed.

"Oh, okay Mr. Bren," Myles replied.

"Let's sharpen our steel."

"Ohhhhh," the class said in unison.

"Okay, class, relax. If Mr. Bren gets this answer right, you all will get an A+ on today's pop quiz."

The class got excited and started hyping up Bren.

"Bren are you ready?" Myles asked.

"I'm ready," Bren responded.

"Good! I want you to define kinetic energy and demonstrate it for the class," instructed Myles.

Bren laughed with the class and looked confused at the same time.

"No one can help you. I need you to define kinetic energy and demonstrate it for me," Myles repeated.

Bren looked around the class hoping he would find a poster of some sort with the definition of kinetic energy.

"That's not fair Mr. Myles," said Bren.

"Ah, ah, ah. I need you to keep that same energy," Mr. Myles said sarcastically.

The class all laughed.

"Come on B! You got this. I need that A+ bro," yelled one of the other students.

Bren laughed, "Alright, alright. I got y'all. Kinetic energy is something like, in motion, right?" Bren asked.

"What do you mean something like, in motion? Can you elaborate?" Myles asked.

"It's the driving force, the prime mover," Bren said.

"Is that correct class?" Myles asked.

The class all said yes.

"So kinetic energy is energy in motion. The energy that a body holds by the quality of being in motion," replied Myles.

Slowly walking around the room, Myles picked up a sheet of paper from Bren's desk and folded into a paper plane. He handed it to Bren and asked him to demonstrate kinetic energy. Bren threw the plane and the class laughed as it gracefully landed on the desk.

"Okay, Bren. I want you to demonstrate kinetic energy to the class?" asked Myles.

"I just did," Bren replied.

"That was my version," rebutted Myles.

"Come on Mr. Myles! Now, I need you to keep that same energy," Bren said with desperation in his voice.

The class all laughed, including Myles.

"Come to the basketball game tonight. My kinetic energy will be displayed on the court. I'm breaking records tonight," said Bren with confidence.

Myles is the head of the science department at Arts and Science Charter School. Myles has a deep passion for science and chemistry. He loves working at the school and teaching his students about the wonderful world of science. Myles teaches science in a nontraditional way and setting. He teaches it hands on, which allows the students to actively participate and retain the information from experience, which is said to be the best teacher.

Myles grew up in a single-parent home with his younger brother Staxx and their mother. His mother worked to provide for him and his brother. She worked at a local restaurant where she was the evening manager. Faith loves her boys. She made sure they had what they needed daily and gave them unconditional love. Faith went without so her sons could go with. She sacrificed her social life and even career to allow her sons to live.

Her mornings consisted of her getting the boys up at 4:30 am and taking them to her sister Yari's apartment who lived across the fence. Myles and Staxx stayed with Brix and Blaze while their mother worked. When Faith took sick, she needed around-the-clock care. She moved from the projects and moved in with her parents, Rosey and Doc.

Years ago...

"Yo, Staxx. Why do you wake up so early! It's 5 o'clock! Go back to sleep," said Myles as he fussed at his brother.

This was every morning. Waking up early and waking everyone else in the house up. Myles and Staxx slept in the last room down the hall to the left. Every grandkid that lived with Doc and Rosey spent some time in the last room to the left.

The room had two twin beds side by side with a window on the left wall. There was no TV in the room, thanks to Blaze. Myles had the right side and Staxx had the left side. They had pictures of their favorite basketball player and favorite rapper. Myles' favorite ballplayer was Allen Iverson, and he was a huge Wu-Tang Clan fan. Myles favorite hairstyle was braided on one side and a nappy afro on the other side.

"Myles and Staxx, I want that room clean before you go outside, and check on your mama before heading out," Doc said from the living room.

"Yes, sir," Myles said.

"Sometimes I feel like leaving this place and never coming back. Myles do this! Myles do that! They don't think I need a break," Myles said mumbling, so his granddad didn't hear him.

"I wish mama would have never gotten sick. We would have never moved here!"

"I like it here, it's not that bad," said Staxx.

"Yeah, you like it because you don't have to do anything. I do everything around here," Myles said while making up his bed.

"Whatever," Staxx said cutting his eyes at Myles.

"Where's my *Supreme Clientele* CD?" Myles asked aggressively.

"I don't know! It was on the dresser," snapped Staxx.

Myles walked over to the dresser and put his CD in the CD player. He skipped it to track 3. This was Myles' favorite song on *Supreme Clientele*. He turned it up and started bopping while he cleaned the room.

Doc heard the music and walked down the hall to the room. He peeped in and saw the brothers cleaning up and rapping the song word for word. Doc smiled and shook his head. Faith heard the music and got out of bed and headed to the boys' room.

"Daddy, I'm sorry about this," apologized Faith.

"Girl, leave them boys alone. Let them play their music," insisted Doc.

That was Doc, coming to the rescue of his grandkids. Doc slowly closed the door and walked back to the living room with Faith.

Myles walked over to the CD player and turned the volume down.

"Yo Staxx, you ever wonder about our family in New York?" Myles asked.

"Sometimes I do," Staxx replied.

"I mean for real bruh, we have never met them, and I bet we have some cool cousins up there. We should go," suggested Myles.

"Where? New York?" Staxx asked.

"Yeah, man. I want to meet the other side of our family," said Myles.

"You know Mama would never let that happen," laughed Staxx.

"That's my point. We are eventually going to grow up, and when we do, I'm going to travel the world."

This was typical Myles, very impulsive and living for the moment.

"The closest you're getting to New York is that Ghostface CD. Now let's finish up here so we can head out," said Staxx while turning the music up.

Myles went in the kitchen to take out the trash. On his way to the kitchen his mother was sitting on the chair watching TV with Grandma Rosey. He went over and kissed his mother and grandmother. His Grandma loved the affection that Myles showed her.

"Did you eat breakfast son?" Grandma Rosey asked.

"No ma'am," answered Myles.

"Eat something before you go out in that heat," instructed Grandma Rosey.

"I love the heat; it doesn't bother me," assured Myles.

"Just do what mama tells you to do and stop talking back. Drink a lot of water, too. I don't want you to monkey in that heat," said Faith.

"Mama, why can't I go visit my family in New York," Myles asked.

Faith got silent. After five seconds she replied, "If they wanted to meet you and your brother, they would have sent for y'all. I'm not going out of the way to build a relationship with those people." Faith spoke with bitterness in her voice.

"But Mama they are my family, too," said Myles.

"Don't stand there and argue with your mama. Now sit down and eat," Grandma said firmly.

"Can I take my food and go eat in the library?" Myles asked.

"Yes, son. Go on ahead," answered Doc.

Myles picked up the plate of grits, eggs, and shark and headed out the back door to the library. Staxx came out of the room but stopped in the middle of the hallway when he heard Rosey talking.

"You need to tell that boy the truth, you can't keep hiding what happened. The truth is going to come out. That is his daddy. You can't deny that. You also need to introduce them to their sister and brother, I've seen the young girl plenty of times, she looks just Staxx," Rosey said to Faith.

Staxx walked in the living room where they were sitting and talking.

"Good morning, Mama, good morning Grandma," greeted Staxx.

"Good morning son," the two women said together.

"Where's Myles?" Staxx asked.

"He went to the library with your granddaddy, have some breakfast son," Rosey said.

Staxx sat down to the table and Grandma Rosey fixed him a vast plate of grits, eggs, and shark. Staxx looked at his mother and laughed as if they had an inside joke. Grandma Rosey has a heavy hand when it comes to making a plate. It's looked at as disrespect if you pass on eating once you were offered.

On his way to the library, Myles saw Dax, Breeze, and Fadez outside.

"Grandma made that?" Dax asked.

"Yep. If you want some you better hurry up before Glaze gets in there," Myles said.

The guys took Myles' advice and went in to get some breakfast. Myles went into the library and picked up a book on energy. He sat down at a table and began to eat his breakfast. He skimmed through the pages while he ate his breakfast. The door opened shortly after he got settled in.

"Can I join you?" asked Doc.

"Sure," answered Myles.

"What are you reading?" Doc asked.

"This book on energy, it's pretty cool," replied Myles.

"You know son, God gave me a vision and he placed it on my heart to build this library. I was praying one night about ways I can help you and the rest of my grandkids. God answered my prayers while I was meditating that same day. He told me to build a library and fill it with all types of books. He also told me that this library will be a place where all my grandkids will get inspired and become creative thinkers. They will learn and unlock their energy by reading books, feeding their souls, and minds," shared Doc.

"Most of the energy we use comes from the sun. It is important to have good energy when you come in here. Look around, everything in this library is a representation of positive energy. When you leave this library, you should feel energized just from the energy that it took to build this place. I gave a lot of my energy by building it and it transferred into every book on these shelves."

"Wow. I never looked at it like that. Thanks for explaining that to me," said Myles.

"Just think, when you are down, or sad, you are drawn to the library because it will fill your soul with the energy that you need," Doc further explained.

He handed Myles three tickets. Myles read one of the tickets. It was a round trip ticket leaving from Yamassee, South Carolina train station to Harlem, New York. Myles looked at Doc and Doc confirmed.

"I know you want to meet your father's side of the family and you should. Your mother has her reasons for sheltering you and she's your mother. But I spoke with your other grandmother Butter last week and arranged for you, me, and Staxx to visit them," said Doc.

"Really?" Myles asked in disbelief.

"Yes, son. We are going to go when school is out," Doc replied.

Myles was excited that he was finally going to meet the other side of his family.

"Does Staxx know," Myles asked.

"No, not yet. I wanted to tell you first. You can break the news to him," Doc said with a smile on his face.

Myles ran out of the library to spread the gospel to his brother. Doc got up from the table and picked up the book that Myles was reading. It was *Managing Kinetic Energy*. Doc smiled and placed the book on the shelf.

Later that night Myles was lying in his bed thinking about his trip to New York. He smiled as he thought about meeting his New York family for the first time and what he would say.

"Staxx, Staxx. I should have known you were sleeping," whispered Myles.

He turned from his side onto his back and gazed at the ceiling. Myles started thinking about his father in prison. I wonder what he's doing now, Myles said to himself. He continued to focus on his father and felt a feeling that he had never felt before. He felt a connection!

"What was that?" Myles said, frightened.

Myles felt his body to see if he was dreaming. He jumped out of his bed and looked around. Staxx was still sleeping.

"I'm tripping. I'm tripping," he whispered to himself. His body jerked and for a second, he saw beams of light. Myles went to his bed and sat on the edge; he rubbed his head with both hands to remain calm. His body jerked again, pushing him on the floor to the other side of the room. He slowly stood up and saw a black greyish fog that trailed his movement from the bed to the where he was.

"God, what is going o..." Myles said before his physical form left the room.

The black fog unhurriedly vaporized in the room. Myles opened his eyes and saw light speed and a metal door in his comprehension. Whoosh! He went through the door as if he was a ghost!

His breaths were heavy as he tried to calm down. He looked around and only saw the inside of his eyelids. He used his hands for his eyes and felt a brick wall. He walked around what seemed to be a small, constricted room with brick walls.

"Where am I?" he cried out. "Staxx! Staxx!"

"Who's there?" a voice said in the dark, brick-walled room.

Myles stopped and remained silent.

"Who's there?" the man said again.

Myles heard the man getting up and fumbling to turn on a light. Myles heard a switch; a small light came from a desk lamp. He backed up when he saw the man standing on the other side of the room about six feet away.

"Myles?" the man asked, confused. The man looked startled to see Myles in the room with him.

Myles rubbed his eyes. "Dad? Is it really you?" Myles asked.

"Yes! It's really me," his dad said as he rushed to Myles and hugged him.

Myles embraced his dad with love.

"How did you get here son?" he asked.

"I don't know," answered Myles.

"My boy, let me look at you," Grip said.

"How's your mama and your brother doing?"

"They're straight," Myles said.

Grip was in solitary confinement. He was confused as to how Myles got into the cell.

"Son, who let you in here?" he asked.

Myles didn't know what to say because he thought it was a dream.

"I was in my bed at Grandpa and grandma house, and I started feeling strange, my body started feeling light. Next thing I know I'm here with you. Myles explained to his father.

Grip didn't believe any of it; however, he was happy to see his son.

"Did the Feds send you here to try and make me snitch? You know your daddy ain't no rat," said Grip.

Grip pulled Myles to him and started checking under his clothes for a wire.

"What are you doing?" said Myles in a confused tone.

Grip was speechless. He went to the edge of his bed and sat down.

"This is weird. I don't understand it," he said.

Myles had a lot on his mind. He didn't know where to start or what to ask.

"Why did you leave us?" he said, staring at his dad.

"Your mama and I were young and in love. We got married at an early age. We were both too young for such a commitment. I never wanted to live down south son, I'm a city boy. You know I really tried hard to get your mama to move up here with me. She just felt like she needed to be close to her family," Grip began to explain.

"How did you get the name Grip?" inquired Myles.

Grip laughed as he started to explain how he used to hustle and always kept a grip of money. Reminiscing about his old days gave him life.

"Yeah, and that's why they call me Big Money Grip. That's what they use to call me. I always kept a grip of money," he said proudly.

"How did you end up in prison?" Myles asked without skipping a beat.

Grip didn't want to talk about it, so he changed the subject.

"How's school and what grade are you in?" he asked his son. "Tell me about Staxx. I miss him so much!"

"Tell me, dad. What did you do to get here?" Myles asked, not allowing his father to distract him.

"What, your mama didn't tell you?" Grip asked sarcastically.

"She said something about you violating probation up here," Myles replied.

Grip looked at Myles and shook his head.

"You really don't know huh? You really don't recall what happened that night?" Grip asked.

Boom, boom, boom!

A loud knock at the door startled Myles.

"Shut up in there and lights out," the C.O. said.

Grip turned the lamp off. Myles felt the same feeling in his body.

"It's happening again," he warned his father.

"What's happening?" Grip asked confused.

"Dad! Dad!"

Whoosh!

Myles teleported from the cell. Flashing lights and light speed grazed his peripheral as his room became his tunnel vision.

Whoosh!

Grayish-black fog slowly evaporated as Myles looked around the room. Staxx was asleep and Myles was totally confused but he knew it was not a dream. He went and sat on his bed trying to make sense of what just took place. Myles dropped to his knees and started praying.

"God I'm scared. Please help me, God. Father, please help me!" Myles cried out.

He slowly stood up from the floor and noticed a bright light shining outside through his window. He walked over to the window holding up his arm to block the bright light. Myles opened the curtain, and a small ball of light was levitating.

A voice outside said: *"This light will guide you when you teleport. Trust in your ability. It is A gift from me to you. Use it wisely."*

Myles opened the window to reach out for the ball of light. The light slowly floated into his open hands as he welcomed it. The circular light gradually interconnected in him. He turned around and Staxx was looking at him.

Before they could say anything, Myles teleported out the room, leaving behind a dark purple fog. Staxx jumped out of the bed.

"Myles! Myles!" he yelled.

Staxx looked around the room, then he ran to the window and drew back the curtains. He saw Myles outside.

He couldn't believe what he was seeing. Staxx wiped his eyes, Myles was teleporting while he was running around the yard, leaving behind a dark purple fog.

Present Day...

Myles walked in the school gym and saw the boys' basketball team warming up and doing shooting drills. The gym was packed on both sides, with the visiting team supporters and home team supporting their Disciples. He walked over to the bleachers and found a seat with one of his co-workers, Alisa.

"What's up, Alisa? Is someone sitting her?" he asked.

"No. Have a seat and keep me company," she said with laughter.

Some of the students from Myles' class saw them sitting together and started giggling and laughing. They both turned around and saw the students laughing.

"You two have great chemistry," one of the students said.

"Thank you," Myles said while laughing.

The shot clock buzzer went off as the game was beginning to start. Both teams met in the center of the court for the jump ball. Bren, the student from Myles' class, looked around. He made eye contact with Myles and waved. Bren was ecstatic to see Myles at the game. He was the starting shooting guard for the home team, The Disciples. Seeing Myles at the game gave him the energy that he needed to perform to the best of his ability.

"I think you just made that young man's day," said Alisa.

"Who Bren? Yeah, that's one of my students. I told him I would come to his game tonight. Let's go, Bren," Myles yelled out as Bren made the first shot of the game.

Bren looked at Myles and threw up a three-pointer sign.

The buzzer sounded for halftime. The score was 50 to 45; the home team was down.

"Excuse me, I'm going to step out to make a call. Would you like something from the concession stand?" asked Myles.

"A bottled water is fine, thank you," said Alisa.

Myles walked out to the concession stand and bought a bottled water and a snack. He pulled out his phone and called his brother.

"Yo," answered Staxx.

"What's good Staxx?" Myles asked.

"Nothing much bro. Just washing some clothes," answered Staxx.

"Word. I'm at the school basketball game right now but I will be there afterwards," Myles said.

"No problem. I'll be here when you get here," replied Staxx.

Myles headed back in the gym in enough time for the 3rd quarter to start. He handed the bottled water to Alisa and opened his snacks. As the game went on Myles and Alisa talked about their love for science and natural healing plants. Before they knew it, the game had made it to the fourth quarter with the score tied 60 to 60.

Everyone was on the edge of their seats and enjoyed the competitive nature of both teams, being that they were rivals. The teams exchanged buckets and the score went back and forth.

"So, what's an intelligent grounded sweet lady like you doing single?" asked Myles flirting.

Alisa laughed.

"Is that a real question or a compliment?" she asked.

"Both," Myles answered.

"I'm single because most men are intimidated by my independence or are just corny," Alisa said. They both laughed.

"Best hip-hop group?" Myles asked out of the blue.

"The Legendary Roots Crew," she said expeditiously.

"I would argue that with Wu-Tang, just for the simple fact Black Thought is the only MC in the group," joked Myles.

"Best hip-hop band hands down."

"Best female MC?" countered Alisa.

"For me, I would have to go with Rapsody, *"Laila's Wisdom"* is a classic album," replied Myles.

"What do you know about Rapsody?" Alisa asked.

"I feel your energy, it's coming through. Took me a century, to get next to yooooou," Myles sung.

Alisa started laughing.

"Stick to teaching science and chemistry," she joked.

They both laughed as they made eye contact. Their energy was necessary.

The referee blew the whistle.

"Shooting foul, number 24. Two shots!"

Both teams lined up as the center from the visiting team walked to the free-throw line.

"Two shots," the ref repeated as he bounce passed the ball to the center.

The home team fans started stomping on the bleachers and making noise. He dribbled the ball twice and shot the ball softly. The noise in the gym elevated and quickly decreased when the ball went through the goal and touched the bottom of the net.

"One shot," the ref said as he bounce passed the ball to the center.

Again, he took two dribbles and release a soft touch shot that silenced the home team fans. The Disciples coach signaled the ref for a full timeout. The score was 68-66, Disciples down with only 10 seconds left in the game.

Bren looked over at Myles and Myles signaled him to relax.

During the timeout, the coach drew up a play that would allow for one shot. Everyone knew the ball was going to Bren, he was hot.

The whistle blew! The ball was inbounded and passed to Bren. Bren looked at the shot clock with six seconds remaining. A layup would send the game into overtime and a three could win it.

Bren drove to his strong side and was blocked off with a double team, keeping his dribble alive. The center for the Disciples set a pick that Chase, the shooting guard, went around. Bren jumped to take a shot and both defenders jumped with him. As he reached his highest height, he looked to his left and saw Chase open in the corner behind the three-point line.

"3! 2!" the crowd counted down!

Bren faked the shot and dished it to Chase! Chase caught the ball and quickly released it, imitating Steph Curry.

"1!" The crowd counted down.

The ball soared through the air and everyone in the gym stood up. Swish!

The buzzer went off! The Disciples pulled it off. The home team side of the gym stampeded the court and "Dreams and Nightmares" played by Meek Mill.

The entire gym sang,

"Hold up wait a minute! Y'all thought I was finished!"

Myles and Alisa both were singing along in excitement. Chase became an overnight celebrity from that shot. Everyone had their phones out taking videos and pictures.

"I really enjoyed myself tonight," Alisa said to Myles.

"I did, too. You are pretty cool. Listen, I know this cool spot where they play the best hip-hop music after hours. Would you like to join me sometime?" Myles asked.

"When you say the best hip-hop music, who are you referring to?" Alisa asked jokingly.

"*The Roots and Erykah Badu will* be performing *You Got Me next week,*" answered Myles.

"You got me huh," Alisa asked. "Give me your phone."

Myles handed his phone, and she called her phone.

"Call me," she said as she handed back his phone.

"And you need to get a case for this phone," she joked.

Myles laughed as he placed his phone in the inside of his jacket. He gave her a hug and told her that he would be in touch.

Myles walked outside and waited to congratulate Bren and the rest of the team on their win. The school parking lot was filled with students and adults. The players trickled out of the side door of the gym and went on with their night. Bren came out of the door and immediately walked over to Myles.

"You really embraced your inner mamba tonight," joked Myles.

Bren laughed.

"Yeah, I was hot tonight. Did you see that pass at the end though? My boy Chase was wet out there."

"You had me scared for a minute when I saw that double team closing in on you," Myles said.

"I knew Chase was coming the entire time. You really don't think I was going to force that shot, do you?" Bren asked.

"You made a great decision at a great time," Myles said.

Chase walked out the side door and started walking to the side of the building.

"Hey Cee! Are you walking home?" Bren asked.

"Yeah," answered Chase.

"Okay, hold up," Bren yelled back.

"Mr. Myles, I'll see you tomorrow. I'm going to walk with Cee."

"I can take you guys home, you don't have to walk," offered Myles.

"Okay cool, Cee hold up. Mr. Myles is going to give us a ride," Bren said.

Chase walked over to Myles and Bren and said, "Good evening Mr. Myles."

"Good game tonight Chase. Where did you learn to shoot like that?" Myles asked.

"This guy right here, we've been friends since elementary school and playing ball together for the longest," Chase said.

They got in the car and Myles pulled out of the parking lot.

"Where are your parents?" Myles asked the boys.

"My mama is working tonight," answered Bren.

"My mom is home with my baby sister and my dad is working," replied Chase.

"Well, call your mother and let her know I'm bringing you home," Myles instructed.

Chase pulled out his phone and called his mother.

"Hey, mom. Yes, ma'am, we won tonight. Wait, how did you hear that so fast? It was awesome. Bren passed to me, and I was wide open," Chase explained.

Chase's mom began to talk his ear off and not let him get a word in. He finally interrupted her.

"Mom, mom. I know but I called to let you know that Mr. Myles is dropping me off home. Yes, Bren is with me. He's right here. Okay, mom. I'll see you soon, yes, I have my key! Love you, too. Good-bye. Uggggh," Chase grunted as he hung up the phone.

Bren and Myles laughed at him.

"Man, Mr. Myles I didn't know you were riding like this," Bren said impressed with Myles' car.

Myles laughed. "It gets from point A to B."

"Yeah, in 0 to 3 seconds," said Bren.

Chase and Bren laughed.

"We live on the same street so you can drop us off at the beginning of the road," Bren said.

"Okay. No problem." Myles replied.

Myles switched his radio to his CD player and "Liberation" by Outkast featuring Cee-Lo and Erykah Badu came on.

The boys started nodding their heads and vibing to the song. Myles looked in his rearview mirror and caught a glimpse of them.

"Y'all feeling that?" Myles asked.

"Yeah, who is this?" Bren asked.

"This is Outkast. The song is titled "Liberation" from their album *Aquemini*," replied Myles.

"Aquemi who?" said Bren.

"Aquemini," Myles repeated.

"That's dope," confirmed Bren.

"Check it out when you get some time. One of the best albums ever created," Myles said.

"Mr. Myles, you are coming up to our street. You can let us out at the stop sign," instructed Chase.

Myles pulled up to the curb and stopped. Bren and Chase got their things and stepped out of the car.

"I'll see you tomorrow in class Mr. Myles," said Bren.

"Thank you, sir, for the ride," thanked Chase.

"No problem. I'll see you fellas later," affirmed Myles.

Myles did a U-turn and proceeded to leave the neighborhood. He stopped at a stop sign about a mile from where he dropped the boys off from and saw two white males running. When they saw Myles, they split up and ran in two different directions. Myles looked back in his rearview mirror and saw blue lights flashing from about a quarter-mile away. Myles pulled off slowly and took a left on a street.

"Bren," Myles said to himself.

Myles got out of the car and ran to the street where he dropped the boys off.

"Check your IG bro. I bet it's lit from tonight's game," Bren said laughing.

Chase and Bren pulled out their phone and started checking the timeline.

"Yooo! He recorded the entire timeout session," Chase said.

The boys watched the last few seconds of the game. Bren commentated the last shot. "Terry inbounds the ball, he drives to his right, a double team meets him there, and it looks like he's in trouble. Vince sets a strong pick that frees up Chase! Bren dishes it to Chase for one shot behind the three-point line. He shoots... Nothing but net," Bren said as he ran in a circle around Chase.

Chase laughed.

"That was pretty good. When you retire from the league you can do play by play for the playoffs."

"You really think I can make it to the league?" Bren asked with a serious undertone.

"Heck yeah broski," Chase replied.

"I really appreciate that Cee," thanked Bren.

They did their signature handshake and followed by saying broskis for life.

"Hold it right there," an officer said approaching the guys from the front. Bren looked behind him and thought about running.

"Hands up!"

Chase and Bren both held their hands up.

"Don't move! Do not move! I have two black males engaging in suspicious activities," said the officer into his radio. The officer stereotyped both boys.

"What are you talking about?" asked Chase.

"Be quiet Cee! Just keep your hands up," pleaded Bren.

"Request for backup, a request for backup," the officer said into his radio.

Chase's phone started vibrating while it was in his hand.

Myles heard the officer yelling, "Keep your hands up!"

He cut between two homes and saw the boys standing with their hands up. Another officer arrived on the scene to assist.

Chase's phone started vibrating again. He looked at his phone and then shots were fired at the boys.

Myles ran from between the houses and quickly teleported. "Liberation" played in his head as he moved quickly through one portal to another.

He grabbed both boys by their team warmup jackets. Myles held on to each boy's arm and started to teleport as the officers emptied their clips.

Myles felt the life leaving from one of the boys as the boy exhaled his final breath, Myles lost his grip once the boy's soul departed his body. His body fell from the active teleportation face down on the pavement.

Lights from all the houses in the neighborhood turned on. The two officers slowly walked to the body with their guns pointed to him. People started coming out of their homes to witness what was going on.

"Stand back," one of the officers yelled to a middle-aged black man.

The officer saw the name Disciples on the back of the jacket. He slowly kicked the body over and saw a phone vibrating with an incoming call from Dad. Chase's blue eyes were wide open with a stare of injustice smeared on his face. The officers started freaking out.

"Stand back, stand back," they instructed the crowd as people came closer to the body and started noticing that it was Chase.

A middle-aged white lady came to the body holding a little baby in one arm and cell phone in the other hand. She looked at the body lying helpless on the pavement with his eyes wide open.

"Noooo! What have you done?" she screamed. The baby started crying as Chase's mom dropped to the pavement and consoled his body.

Another white officer arrived on the scene and slowly walked to the body. When the officer saw the lady holding the body on the ground he started tearing up. He too dropped to the pavement and started crying.

The two officers that killed Chase attempted to explain what happened to the arriving officer, Chase's father. "You killed my son," Chase's father screamed.

"We didn't know! We thought he had a gun, and, and there was another kid with him that had a gun," the officer said.

Myles and Bren listened to the officer as he tried to explain murdering an unarmed innocent teenager. Myles slowly backed out from between the houses and teleported with Bren.

"I don't have a gun," Bren whispered to Myles as they opened the car door.

"I know you don't. Let me make a call, she'll know what to do," said Myles.

He took out his phone and went to his favorites.

"Hello," a sleepy female voice answered.

"Hey, Kenya. It's Myles. I need your help cuz," Myles said.

Chapter 12:

BOOK OF STAXX

Years ago...

A red compressed soda can was mounted firmly on the back tire of a bicycle. Blaze came to a stop by jerking the handlebar to the left and letting one foot off the petal. The back tire dug into the dirt as the bike skidded to a stop.

"Yo! Hurry up!" he said while looking back as the dust cleared.

Myles pulled up on his bike, breathing heavily.

"Slow down," he said.

"Where is your brother?" Blaze asked.

"He was right behind me," Myles replied while looking back.

He saw Staxx walking on the side of his bike, slowly pushing it by the handlebars.

"Hurry up," Myles yelled from a distance.

Staxx lifted his head up and wiped the sweat from his face with his shirt. Staxx slowly approached Blaze and Myles, drenched in perspiration using his shirt for a sponge to absorb the moisture from his face.

"I can't ride any more fellas. I'm tired," Staxx said.

"We almost there," Myles said.

"My head is hurting, and it feels like it's ringing," Staxx replied.

They looked at him and knew he was hurting for real, so they came up with a plan.

"Okay, leave your bike in the bushes. You can ride on the handle-bar, and we'll just ride out like that. Once we get to Aunt Beck's, we can get what we need, get you a Gatorade and then come back for your bike," said Myles as he quarterbacked the plan.

"Yeah, whatever, let's just go," Staxx said distressed.

He slowly got on the handlebars of Myles' bike and Blaze hid Staxx's bike between two bushes. They started riding to the store. It was hot. The temperature was in the high 90s and the humidity was scorching. The sun's rays heated the pavement, and the heat was visibly rising from the sidewalk.

Blaze led the way while Myles and Staxx followed close behind. Staxx's headache became unbearable as he started to black in and out.

"Stop the bike, please stop," Staxx said.

"We almost there, hold on," Myles replied.

Staxx started hearing voices from other people. He looked around and saw people and other kids playing. The voices got louder in Staxx's head.

"You hear that?" he asked his brother.

Myles didn't reply, he kept riding to keep up with Blaze. Myles felt Staxx leaning back on the handlebars and that he had shifted all his weight. Myles pressed the brakes and stopped.

"Staxx! Staxx!" yelled Myles trying to wake up his brother. Blaze looked back and saw Staxx slumped back on the handlebars. He quickly jumped off and ran to them. Myles and Blaze lifted Staxx off the bike and laid him down. He was breathing but he wasn't responding to them.

"Let's get him in the store," said Myles.

Myles lifted Staxx's upper body while Blaze lifted his lower body. Blaze opened the door with one hand and screamed. "Someone help us!"

Aunt Beck stood behind the counter, wearing a long indigo color house coat.

"What's wrong with that boy?" she asked.

"I think he passed out," Blaze said.

"Lock that doe Egypt," Aunt Beck ordered. A young girl ran to the door and turned the "Open" sign to "Closed".

"Bring him back yuh," said Aunt Beck as she directed the boys. She went in the back of the store; it was dark and hot.

"Egypt, go call yo' granddaddy and tell 'em come yuh. Lay 'em on this bed right cha," Aunt Beck said.

Myles and Blaze carefully laid Staxx on the bed. Aunt Beck looked at Staxx and said, "This Faith boy."

She grabbed a deep wooden bowl and filled it with cold water. She then placed a rag in it to let it soak. She wiped his body down with rubbing alcohol and cold water.

Staxx heard voices in his head that sounded like several people chattering in Hebrew. Aunt Beck continued to rub Staxx down with the water to cool him off. Staxx's body became overheated.

"Y'all churn go outside and look for ya' granddaddy. When yuh see 'em, send 'em in yuh," Aunt Beck said.

"Yes, ma'am," Myles replied.

Myles and Blaze ran out of the room and Egypt followed behind them.

Staxx's arm fell to the floor. Aunt Beck placed her ear to his chest to hear his heart. She heard nothing.

"Help God," she said.

Staxx started comprehending the voices in the Hebrew language that was in his head. One voice drowned out all the other voices that he was hearing.

"My son. Focus on me, do not be distracted by the other voices. I am the one and only true God. I have blessed you with supreme powers of the mind. here, drink the juice from the Buluu Herb, embrace your powers. I will always be with you."

Aunt Beck went to a chair to sit down to gather her thoughts. She went into a deep meditation to gain guidance from God. About 15 minutes passed and she heard a soft whisper that said, "*Find the Innergium.*"

She got up from the chair and went to a shelf with several flowerpots. Doc arrived at the store, opened the door, and went to Staxx.

"He alright Beck?" he asked with concern.

"No, but he will be. Lock that doe," said Aunt Beck.

She then fumbled and moved several flowerpots that were lined up horizontally. A medium size white ceramic pot was kept obscured on the backrow. She carefully grasped the pot with both hands, admiring the dark blue soil that pulsated. Aunt Beck gently pulled out the herb that was nesting in the magical soil. The herb was scenic, the lime green petals gleamed with a natural shine. The stem was also green while the indigo color roots moved like spider legs. She rinsed the soil off the roots that left blue residue in the sink. She placed the herb in a mortar and started grinding it with the pestle. Doc marveled as the clear water transitioned to an indigo dye.

"Lift aye head up," she instructed Doc.

Doc lifted Staxx's head up and Aunt Beck opened his mouth and poured the blue liquid in Staxx's mouth.

"*Wake up my son,*" the voice said to Staxx.

Staxx started coughing as the blue drink went down his throat. He slowly opened his eyes and saw Aunt Beck and Doc by his side. Aunt Beck started praising God for the miracle she witnessed.

"You a special young man," she said to Staxx.

Staxx told Aunt Beck thank you in his mind.

"Thank you, God," Staxx heard Aunt Beck's thought.

"Thank you, God! Thank ya," she yelled.

Staxx looked at Doc with water in his eyes.

"It's okay son. He is real," Doc said.

Staxx started to cry.

Knock, knock!

Staxx looked at the door and a sensational power travel through his mind. Flowerpots started falling from the shelves and the historical Gullah art fell from the wall. Staxx heard a voice that said, *"Focus."*

He turned his focus to the door and that same voice said, *"Block out all distractions and focus on one. Unlock and open the door."*

The locked knob slowly turned vertical, and the door opened all the way until it gently touched the wall. Aunt Beck and Doc looked at Staxx. Myles and Blaze stood outside of the room.

Present day...

"Psalm, Pt. 4" by John Coltrane played in the background while Staxx packed a duffel bag. The room was neatly organized.

Staxx walked to his closet and grabbed two pair of sneakers. He walked out of the room to his living area. On the walls were art from Tony Burns and Sonja Evans. He placed his bag by the door and his sneakers. He walked in his office and turned the light on. A bookshelf filled with books stood aligned in order by categories.

Staxx walked over to his vinyl collection and removed the current record that was spinning and placed in back in the cover. He placed the record back on the shelf between other records. He skimmed through the records and grabbed one off the shelf. He took the vinyl out of its cover and gently placed it on the turntable. He placed the needle on the record, relaxing sounds of cracking played, and a soulful voice enter by saying.

"Fellas I'm ready to get up and do my thing."

James Brown's "Get Up" played while he nodded his head and took books from his shelf and put them in a black backpack. He started dancing in the office and walked over to a mirror and looked at his face.

Staxx looked at the scar on his forehead and rubbed it. He stopped dancing as the music played softly in the back. The music slowly faded out as he reminisced on the sequence of events that led up to the scar on his forehead.

Years ago, A teenage Staxx and Myles were walking from Brad's Barbershop.

"There they go," yelled a boy from the rival basketball team.

"Be cool. I'm not running from these punks," Myles said.

A pickup truck slammed on brakes and three boys jumped out.

"What's up with all that tough talk now, Myles?" the passenger side boy said.

"What's up?" Myles replied.

"Let's just go," urged Staxx.

Mac, the kid that had beef with Myles, started walking around the brothers while the other two boys stood in front of Staxx and Myles. Mac continued to taunt Myles by talking tough. Staxx turned around quick as he felt Mac reaching in his pocket. Myles turned around too. The other two boys got closer to Myles and Staxx, invading their space.

"Yo, back up off of me," Myles said to the two boys.

"Shut up before I stab you punk," Mac said as he pulled out a knife.

Mac stood about three feet from Myles and Staxx while the other two boys stood behind them.

"Knock this punk out," one of the boys said while pushing Staxx in the back.

Mac lunged at Myles with the knife, Staxx moving quickly from the push headed straight in Mac's direction. Staxx gestured his hand in a motion without touching Mac, the knife dropped from his hand.

Staxx's forehead collided with Mac's mouth. They both fell to the ground. Mac was holding his mouth and screaming. Myles picked up the knife and turned to the other two boys that stood behind him.

Staxx forcefully pointed at the boys with his hand, and they went flying back about ten feet. Mac got up with a mouth full of blood and mumbled.

"Let's get out of here."

They ran to the truck and sped off, leaving Myles and Staxx behind. Myles dropped the knife and went to his brother's aid.

"Don't move, don't move," Myles said.

Mr. Brad ran across the street when he noticed the boys outside on the ground. Mr. Brad was a big round man, with silky, white, wavy hair. He knew the boys well. He would let Faith credit haircuts and pay him once she got paid. Sometimes he wouldn't take her money because he knew she was a single mother trying to raise two boys.

"What happened?" Mr. Brad asked.

"We got into it with some guys," answered Myles.

He looked at the knife on the ground. There was no blood on the knife, but Staxx forehead was covered in blood.

"Is that yours?" he asked Myles.

"No sir," Myles replied.

"Hand it to me and help me pick him up," Mr. Brad said to Myles.

He then carried Staxx in his arms to the front door of his house. Staxx heard James Brown playing in the background as Mr. Brad ordered his wife to get a towel.

He laid Staxx on the couch and wiped the blood from his face. Myles stood by his side as they noticed a chipped tooth engraved in his forehead.

"Can you hold this towel on your head?" Mr. Brad asked Staxx.

Staxx nodded and grabbed the towel.

"I'm taking you to the emergency room. Let's go! Baby, let the customers in the shop know I have an emergency. Take all of their names and have them come back tomorrow for free cuts," he asked of his wife.

Mr. Brad, Staxx, and Myles headed to the hospital in a Cadillac. Myles sat in the back of the car with his brother as Mr. Brad drove furiously, even running red lights to get to his destination. Staxx remained calm and could only think about the smell of the towel. The cloth smelled as if it was at the bottom of the hamper of wet clothes and was used to dry someone's boonkey. Staxx didn't complain about the smell, but he looked at his brother and rubbed the towel in his face to give him a whiff of the stench. Myles quickly moved the towel out of his face and he and Staxx laughed. When they arrived at the ER, Mr. Brad called Faith to inform her of the incident.

Staxx continued to stare in the mirror at the scar on his head while the James Brown record played.

"Rest in Peace Mr. Brad," he said. The front doorknob turned, and the door opened.

"Staxx where you at?" a voice said.

Staxx walked out of the office and saw Myles.

"What's good?" Staxx asked.

"I just witnessed a murder," Myles said still in shock. He started rambling and speaking fast. Staxx heard bits and pieces of the story and couldn't grasp it all. Staxx closed his eyes and communicated with Myles.

"Calm down, calm down," he transferred the words to Myles.

Myles heard Staxx's voice in his head.

"Yo! Don't do that! That's some freaky stuff," Myles barked at his brother.

"Are you calm now?" Staxx asked.

"Yes. Let me have a seat," Myles said.

They walked over to the kitchen and sat around the island. Myles started explaining the sequence of events leading up to Chase getting shot down.

"Where is Bren now?" Staxx asked.

"He's home," answered Myles.

"So, you left the crime scene?" Staxx asked, getting upset.

"No, no, no. I went down to the station with Bren and his family. Kenya and her team met us there and stayed with the family.

Staxx got up and walked to a window. He looked out the window and saw a grey car parked at a distance from his house. The car pulled off.

"Did anyone follow you here," Staxx asked.

"Nah, I'm pretty sure I wasn't being followed," Myles said.

Staxx yawned, as he looked at the clock on the wall that read 2:30 am.

"That's a lot to process for one night. We need to get some sleep, are you still riding with me to BFT?" Staxx asked.

"Yes, I should be fine. I spoke to Kenya about that, and she said it's okay. I'm going to meet with her and Bren's family in the morning," answered Myles.

"So… Bren saw your powers," Staxx asked.

"I had no choice. I had to do something," Myles replied.

"Get some rest bro," Staxx said as he hugged his brother.

He walked out of the kitchen and headed upstairs to his bedroom.

Myles stayed downstairs and thought about Chase and Bren. He took out a sheet of paper, a pen, and wrote a note.

I'M HEADED OUT, I NEED TO CHECK ON A FEW THINGS BEFORE WE LEAVE. DON'T WORRY I'M OKAY. CALL ME WHEN YOU GET UP. MYLES.

He placed the note on the refrigerator, turned the lights off, and headed out. Staxx's eyes opened from the door closing. Myles walked out of the house and looked around. He walked to his car and got in. He looked in his rearview mirror and noticed a grey car parked a few houses down.

"Who is this?" he said quietly to himself.

He started the car and put it into drive. He slowly made a U-turn in the grey car's direction. Myles rolled down his window to see if someone was in the car. He pulled up alongside of the car and looked in from his seat. Myles took his right hand off the wheel and grabbed a CD from his vast collection. As he held the CD, a blue energy transferred from his hand and turned the CD light blue.

Myles charged the CD up with the energy from his hand as he anticipated to release it at whoever was in the car. Myles slowly drove up to where he could see the back of the car. The license plate read SS-2NG. He took out his phone and took a picture of the plate and slowly drove off. Myles threw the CD in the air. He looked up as the trail of blue light ascended in the sky and illuminated the street.

The alarm on the Smart-Watch on Staxx's wrist went off. He sat up in his bed. He looked at his wrist and the time was 4:44 am. Staxx looked up at the moonlight as he prayed and meditated for about 30 minutes. He smiled once he received confirmation.

He took out his phone and send a group text to the fellas. His morning routine was in progress. Staxx opened the door and looked outside. The morning was young, and the sun was making its way to its destination.

"Something feels different this morning," he thought to himself. He stepped back in the house and closed the door.

At 8:15 am, his eyes closed, and the sound of an engine started. Scarface's "That's Where I'm At" faded in as the top of the car slowly opened as he drove to the office. He engaged his telekinesis ability.

A Pad opened and powered on. The home screen displayed a background picture of the back of a small brick house, two large oak trees, and a long gas tank. As he thought of his agenda, the words appeared on his Pad.

Staxx pulled into the parking lot and parked. His Pad had two pages of notes. He gathered his things and headed inside. He walked in and saw his assistant, Lauryn.

"Good morning, Lauryn," Staxx said as he greeted her.

"Good morning, Staxx," she replied.

Lauryn had moved down from DC to relocate and start a career in counseling.

"How was your evening?" Staxx asked.

"It was cool. I went to a high school basketball game with a friend. I saw your brother there," she said.

"One of the players got gunned down after the game by a police officer," Staxx informed her.

"Oh no! What happened?" Lauryn asked.

Staxx walked to the front desk, picked up the remote control and turned the TV on to watch the news.

"That reminds me, I need to call Myles," Staxx said as he walked back to his office to call his brother.

Meanwhile, Lauryn watched the news in pure terror.

"An unarmed white teen was gunned down last night by the hands of an on-duty officer from what seems to be a case of mistaken identity. This teen's night ended tragically as he was walking home from a basketball game. A statement has not been issued by the department. This case hits home for the department because the teen that got gunned down is the son to one of our very own officers."

Lauryn walked back to where Staxx was. He held up his index finger to signal Lauryn to give him a minute.

"Okay. How's Bren doing?" Staxx asked.

"He's shook up but he's being strong. The basketball team is rallying to go and protest in front of the police department today at noon. You know Staxx, the tables have turned for them. Sometimes they must experience pain and hurt to change. They've been gunning down our little kings for years! They thought Chase was another black boy. I am sorry that Chase loss his life, but I truly think this will put a spotlight on the police department and gunning down unarmed black males. You know Chase's father is an officer. This will bring attention to their profiling and unjust behaviors towards young black and brown men," shared Myles.

"I agree with you 100%, let me get back to work. I'll hit you up later," said Staxx as him and Myles said good-bye.

Staxx walked out and Lauryn was still watching the news. The news was reporting from the community where Chase was shot and killed.

Neighbors were telling the reporters about Chase and their experience knowing him. That he was a great kid, and he didn't deserve that.

"One guy shared that Chase scored the winning shot last night. Is this what it will take to bring attention to all of the unarmed black teens getting murdered?" Lauryn asked.

"My brother said the same thing. Now they can experience empathy," Staxx said.

"Are you ready for your 9:30? You have Ricky Beam, then at 1:00 pm you have Paige Davenport," Lauryn stated.

"Okay. Do we have any updates from Mr. Beam?" Staxx asked.

"Last week his barriers were that he went back to his ex," Lauryn said.

"That's right. Just send him back when he gets here. How's school going for you?" questioned Staxx.

"One more semester, so it's really my grind time. I do have one professor that's very demanding and has been a pain in my, boonkey?" Lauryn said, trying to speak the Gullah language.

Staxx laughed with her.

"That will prepare you for this line of work. Just put it on cruise control from here. You're going to be running this office soon. Lauryn's counseling services. Sounds good, right," Staxx said holding his hands in the air as if outlining her future office sign.

Lauryn chuckled and Staxx went back to his office to prepare for his session with Mr. Beam. Once in his office, Staxx turned on one of his favorite jazz albums. Lauryn knocked on the door and Staxx told her to come in.

"Do you have a minute?" she asked.

"Sure. What's up?" asked Staxx.

"I'm thinking about taking some time to go and visit Que and Night," she said.

"You know, I'm actually meeting up with them this weekend in BFT. Would you like to come?" invited Staxx.

"That would be great, I can surprise them," Lauryn said with a smile on her face.

"Cool. Myles and I are leaving after my last appointment today. If you want to, we can swing by your place so you can pack a bag, after our last session, and go right ahead," said Staxx.

"That sounds great," replied Lauryn.

Staxx felt the need to look after Lauryn and take care of her knowing what she'd been through as a child. When Que and Night made the decision to send Lauryn to college in Charlotte, they asked Staxx to look after her, like a little sister. From that day, Staxx vowed to look after her and keep her safe. Letting Lauryn intern at his practice allowed him to assist her in her career and lead her in the right direction.

Mr. Beam arrived and Lauryn walked him back to the office.

"Staxx and I are glad to see you today," said Lauryn as she welcomed Mr. Beam.

"So much has happened since our last session. I got my juice back, my girl back and feel like I'm on top of the world," Ricky said as he continued to ramble for about three minutes. He was filled with excitement.

"Slow down Ricky. Let's look back to where you were and then walk back to the present. About two months ago, you and your girlfriend separated because she caught you cheating. You felt that you couldn't live without her and wanted to do whatever it took to get her back. She advised that you seek help and show her that you are ready to be in a committed relationship. You started therapy twice a week focusing on your past to answering questions of your behaviors today. Your progress was moderate with minor setbacks," shared Staxx as he summarized with Ricky.

"Wow, it has been two months," said Ricky in disbelief.

"So, you and your friend went out on a date I'm assuming," Staxx asked.

"Yeah Staxx, we went on a date. We had a great time; it was like getting to know her all over again. I was a gentleman and all like you suggested, opening doors and all. I wasn't taught that growing up, so I missed a lot of simple things. She really enjoys the simple things. I really want to thank you for unpacking my entire life, neatly folding my characteristics and values and placing them back in the proper place," Ricky explained.

"So, it sounds like you and your friend are starting a new beginning," Staxx inquired.

"Yes, we are," Ricky confirmed.

"I wanted to show you something," Ricky said as he went in his pocket and pulled out a box.

"I'm going to ask Korinne to marry me. What do you think about that?" asked Ricky.

"Do you feel like you've emptied your tank of lust? Are you ready to fill it up with Korinne's love?" Staxx asked.

"I know that I love her, and I don't want to lose her ever again for my wrong-doings," Ricky said sincerely. Staxx read Ricky's body language and realized that he was telling the truth.

"Well Ricky, I wish you success on your proposal and I think you will be a great husband for Korinne. Keep God first in everything you do. You will be fine," assured Staxx.

"I definitely will, and I will send you an invitation to our wedding. You are a major part of my development as a man. Thank you again," said Ricky as he grabbed Staxx for a hug.

1:30pm...
Lauryn lifted her head out of her book she was studying. A man stood in the front of her. He wore a white T-shirt with black military style pants with black steel toe boots strung tight. He wore a truck driver hat with aviator shades covering his eyes.

"Yes, may I help you, sir?" Lauryn asked.

"I need to see Staxx," the man replied.

"He's in a session right now if you would like to have a seat, I will let him know he has a visitor," Lauryn said as she looked outside the window.

She noticed a grey car in the parking lot. Lauryn looked at him as he walked away. He signaled a guy to come inside. The other guy stepped out of the car from the passenger side. He too was dressed in the same attire as the first guy. The first guy entered back in the office and the second guy followed with his back turned. The guys approached Lauryn and pointed an AR 15 towards her.

"Come from behind the desk now," ordered the man.

Lauryn looked back with fear not knowing if she should follow the man's orders. She slowly walked from behind the desk as the second guy pointed the gun in her face.

The first guy nodded his head at his partner with the AR-15. Lauryn screamed at the top of her lungs! The first guy grabbed Lauryn and covered her mouth and nose with a cloth that instantly knocked her out. He lifted her and threw her across his shoulders and headed out. The other guy inserted a clip. He walked down the hall to Staxx's office and started to spray the office with bullets. He looked at the sign on the door that said "Staxx" and started shooting through the window and the door. The bullets shattered the windows and traveled through the office with finesse and impulsivity.

Click, click. The chamber was empty.

He inserted another clip and continued to spray through the door and windows. The man slowly walked from the office stepping on the shattered glass in the hallway. He opened the office door and slammed it behind him. The sign fell from the force. He ran to the car, opened the passenger door, and jumped in as his partner shifted from park to drive and sped out of the parking lot.

Staxx laid on the floor with his hand touching Mrs. Davenport's ankle. Staxx was covering Mrs. Davenport in a force field, and he placed her in a coma. Staxx was using his telekinesis powers to remove the bullets from entering his flesh, he felt each bullet slowly squeezing its way into his flesh and draining his energy. He knew if he took the focus off the bullets, they would enter his body and rip through all his organs. He also knew if he let his hand fall off Mrs. Davenport that she would wake up and panic.

Staxx thought to reach out to Brix. He closed his eyes. Still focusing on the bullets and Mrs. Davenport, he engaged his telepathy powers to connect with Brix.

Staxx traveled through Brix's mind and removed all the distractions so he would have a clear path to communicate with him.

Brix was on the Homestead, in the library relaxing listening to the *Book of Ryan*. Brix laid on the couch with his headphones on his ears. The music that played through the headphones slowly faded out. Brix opened his eyes and pulled out his phone to see if it was charged; it was. He turned the volume up; no sound came through the headphones.

"Brix," a voice said.

Brix looked around to see who called his name.

"Brix, it's me Staxx," Brix took the headphones off and stood up off the couch.

"Brix, relax, it's me Staxx. I need your help," pleaded Staxx.

"How are you able to talk to me?" Brix asked.

"Focus Brix! Focus! I have bullets that are about to pierce through my body any second!" Staxx yelled at Brix. "I've been ambushed. My powers are draining and I'm not able to move the bullets. I'm losing my energy by the second. I need you to help me," Staxx cried out.

A vision came to Brix, the same vision that occurred in his mind when he was riding with Doc as a teenager.

"Staxx, I saw this happening years ago. I thought about this image for years. What do you need me to do?" Brix asked.

"Use your powers to focus on the vision that you saw. Embrace it. Remove the bullets from my body. Please, Brix! I'm losing my focus," Staxx struggled to get the rest of his thoughts out.

Brix took a deep breath and he focused on the vision. He saw the vision clearly. Bullets gradually piercing through flesh. Brix took a deeper breath and moved his hands in an upward motion to manipulate the bullets. As he moved his hands up, the bullets slowly exited from Staxx's flesh.

Two cars pulled up at the office at the same time. A muscular man got out of a red vehicle and Myles got out of his car.

Myles approached the man.

"Who are you?" he asked the man.

The man didn't say anything and proceeded to walk in the office. He opened the door and Myles followed behind him. They both looked around.

"Paige! Paige!" the man screamed.

Myles ran to Staxx's office, and the man followed him.

They stepped on the shattered glass from the windows in the hallway. Myles looked at the door that was filled with bullet holes.

"No, no, no," he said, starting to panic.

He pushed the door opened. Brix focus disengaged. He looked around at the books in the library, he got up from the sofa and wipe the tears from his eyes. He headed out the door and saw the fellas.

"What's wrong?" Que asked as soon as he saw Brix.

Brix remained silent as he tried to put what just happened together. Dax, Night, Breeze, Fadez, and Blaze all walked towards Brix as he stood with tears in his eyes.

"Come on Brix. What's wrong? What happened?" Que asked again.

"It's Staxx. He's been shot," Brix stumbled to get out.

"What do you mean?" Fadez asked.

"Call Myles! Now!" demanded Breeze.

Myles looked around the office and almost lost it all. He looked at the walls with bullet holes and the desk with broken statues. He looked on the floor and saw his brother.

"Staxx," Myles said as he ran to him. His body was stretched out on the floor.

The man followed behind Myles and ran to Mrs. Davenport.

"Don't talk, don't talk," Myles trying to keep Staxx calm.

Staxx released Mrs. Davenport from the force field as she slowly sat up. Staxx laid on the floor surrounded by bullet shells. His shirt was filled with holes from the bullets that almost entered. Staxx looked at his body and noticed that all the bullets that were penetrating his flesh had dropped to the floor.

"What happened?" Myles asked fighting back tears.

"I don't know," answered Staxx.

Mrs. Davenport slowly stood up with assistance from the man.

"I'm alright Thomas," she said.

"What did you do to my wife?" the man asked.

"Where's Lauryn?" Staxx asked, cutting off Mr. Davenport.

Staxx rushed out of his office in search of Lauryn. Myles' phone rang.

"Yeah," he answered.

"Is Staxx okay?" Breeze asked over his speakerphone.

"Yeah, he's good. I have to find Lauryn," Staxx said as he walked back towards the hallway.

"They got Lauryn," said Myles.

"Who got Lauryn?" Que asked.

"Someone destroyed my office. They took an attempt on my life. Whoever did this took Lauryn," Staxx explained.

"Noooooo!" Night yelled as he took off his shades and looked up to the sky.

A dark shadow illuminated from Night's eyes and covered the sun in totality. The day went dark! A full solar eclipse.

Several men in a warehouse with black cargo pants, black boots, and white T-shirts with the letters SS on their right chest talked indistinctly. A young lady tied up to a chair with tape on her mouth in a dark room slept with her head slumped.

"Lauryn, wake up...Lauryn," a voice echoed.

Lauryn's eyes opened. She heard Doc's voice in her head as footsteps approached her.

The delicate sounds of bristles from a wooden brush slowly stroked the edges of her merlot hue hair. The servant rubbed the Queen's lengthy braids that graced her spine. She stopped brushing and looked at the door.

"My queen, the Souvenir has arrived. It is time," the servant said.

The Queen looked at the servant through the vanity mirror.

"Why is she important to you," the servant inquired.

"God's Souvenir, she has been chosen to bring new life. What is destined can be demolished, once I received the two daggers," The Queen said.

She stood up from the plush bench and held her hand out. An elegant, golden dagger was placed in her palm. The Queen opened her silk robe and placed the dagger in a golden scabbard that was attached to her fitted suit, that embraced her figure. She walked out the room, as the high heels clattered throughout the corridor, alerting her arrival.

THE END

ABOUT THE AUTHOR

Damon Thompson was born and raised in Beaufort, South Carolina. He earned a BS in Human Services at The University of South Carolina at Beaufort, and an MS in Human Services at Capella University. After starting his professional career at Robert Smalls Middle School where he served as a behavioral intervention specialist, he now works with youth and their families to provide multisystemic therapy.

From a young age, Damon loved to create characters and bring them to life. After the birth of his second daughter, he decided to put his creative thoughts into action and begin writing his first novel, which was published in 2019. In his spare time Damon enjoys listening to music from jazz to hip-hop. He also has a passion for the outdoors and nature, as it inspires him to write. He currently resides in North Carolina with his wife and two daughters.

CPSIA information can be obtained
at www.ICGtesting.com
Printed in the USA
LVHW031218080223
738924LV00005B/18